"Welcome to fatherhood."

With a growl, Luke clapped his hat onto the hat rack. "This isn't fatherhood," he said, whirling back to face her. "This is only temporary. No way is this going to be permanent."

"Well, no," Shannon said carefully, taken aback by his vehemence. "You said your sister would be back for the baby."

"That's right." He took a couple of frustrated turns around the room. "Then things will get back to being normal around here."

Meaning lonely, Shannon thought. Even though she knew she should drop the subject, she was compelled to ask, "Don't you ever have plans to be a father, Luke?"

"Heck, no. I like being a bachelor. I like it fine. I'm just not cut out to be a husband or father."

Shannon's heart sank, but this was too interesting not to pursue. "Mind telling me why?"

Dear Reader,

Bachelor Cowboy is the third book in my miniseries
MARRIAGE TIES, about a family of strong women, the
Kellehers. I have already told you the stories of Rebecca,
in *Another Chance for Daddy*, and of Brittnie, in *Wedding Bells*. If
you read these you are ready for Shannon's story. If you are
new to the series, welcome!

In the course of her job, Shannon clashes with sexy but
stubborn Luke Farraday. It seems their differences won't
be resolved until Luke has temporary care of his baby
nephew, and Shannon is the one he turns to for help...

Later this year, look for *Resolution: Marriage*, the story of
Mary Jane, the mother of these three women. Reunited with
her high school sweetheart, she must come to terms with a
secret she's kept for more than twenty-five years.

Be prepared to laugh, and maybe to cry, but certainly to
enjoy the strength and resourcefulness of Rebecca, Brittnie,
Shannon and Mary Jane.

Happy Reading!

Patricia Knoll

Praise for *Wedding Bells*:
"...an engaging tale."
—*Romantic Times*

Books by Patricia Knoll

HARLEQUIN ROMANCE®

3442—TWO-PARENT FAMILY
3502—ANOTHER CHANCE FOR DADDY
3530—WEDDING BELLS

Don't miss any of our special offers. Write to us at the
following address for information on our newest releases.

Harlequin Reader Service
U.S.: 3010 Walden Ave., P.O. Box 1325, Buffalo, NY 14269
Canadian: P.O. Box 609, Fort Erie, Ont. L2A 5X3

Bachelor Cowboy
Patricia Knoll

Marriage
Ties

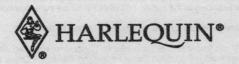

HARLEQUIN®

TORONTO • NEW YORK • LONDON
AMSTERDAM • PARIS • SYDNEY • HAMBURG
STOCKHOLM • ATHENS • TOKYO • MILAN • MADRID
PRAGUE • WARSAW • BUDAPEST • AUCKLAND

RECYCLED PAPER
RECYCLED PAPER

ISBN 0-373-03562-4

BACHELOR COWBOY

First North American Publication 1999.

Copyright © 1999 by Patricia Knoll.

CHAPTER ONE

His backside looked good.

Shannon Kelleher stood beside one of the empty stalls in Luke Farraday's barn and looked up to where he was perched on a huge beam that ran the width of the building. He was inspecting the underside of the roof, and she was honest enough to admit that she was inspecting him.

When she had first seen him, backlit by the June afternoon sun streaming in through the hay door, she'd caught her breath and stared, standing silently in the shadows. She hadn't called out to announce her arrival for fear of startling him. She just wanted to look.

She liked what she saw, long legs, wide shoulders whose muscles rippled and lengthened as he reached up with a hammer in one hand. He was rapping loudly, methodically on the underside of the shingles, which explained why he didn't seem to have heard her drive up.

His other hand was braced against a header joist to keep himself from falling. He was wearing boots, the heels notched over the edge of a beam. That position served to extend his legs and tighten the muscles all the way up.

Nice buns, she thought. Scientifically speaking, of course.

Shannon bit her lip to hide a grin. All right, maybe

that was exaggerating a bit. She couldn't actually *see* the muscles. Besides, human anatomy didn't have a whole lot to do with her job as a range management specialist. Her areas of expertise were soils, grasses and water control. On the other hand, she appreciated anything that nature had put together beautifully.

Nature hadn't exactly been sleeping on the job while assembling Luke Farraday. At least, that's who she thought this man was. There was no one else around.

Shannon admitted that she should be ashamed of herself for ogling the man, especially considering how she hated that kind of thing herself. She had been on the receiving end of sexism more times than she could count and more often in the past year than ever before in her life or career.

Still, she wasn't being lewd and lascivious. It was more like art appreciation, she thought, leaning against the stall railing and crossing her booted ankles. Like viewing Michelangelo's *David*—with a Western theme. The only way it could get any better would be if he took his shirt off.

Besides, she thought, she deserved a little self-indulgent ogling because she'd been sick for a week with a middle-ear infection that had kept her flat on her back in bed. She still felt a little dizzy and weak, but she'd had to get back to work today. Things were piling up. Things that her boss, Wiley Frost, thought only she should resolve.

When Luke Farraday stopped testing the roof and stood staring up, Shannon felt she almost knew what he was thinking. The roof would need to be replaced by winter. The ranch had been allowed to run down by its previous owner, and Luke Farraday had taken on a big job getting the place into shape. Lucky for him, she could help.

Luke reached to place the hammer in his back pocket, and Shannon knew the show was over. She waited until he sat down on the rafter and dangled his feet over the edge before she spoke.

"Mr. Farraday." She stepped out from the shadowed stall, and his head snapped up.

"Who's there?" he barked, leaning over to look. His gaze swept the place until he located her.

Shannon hoped that the irate tone was because she'd startled him. She hugged her clipboard to her chest and walked to stand beneath the rafter where he sat.

When she tilted her head, her long black hair swept her waist. The motion made her ears ring, but she formed a warm smile anyway. "My name's Shannon Kelleher. I'm with the natural resources office. I called your house but couldn't get an answer, so I thought I'd just take a chance and see if you were here."

"I'm here," he said laconically. "What do you want?" As he spoke, he grabbed one of the thick posts that supported the barn roof. It had huge nails driven into it here and there down its length, and he used these as foot and handholds as he made his way to the floor. He moved as easily and gracefully as a trapeze artist from one nail to the next.

Eyes wide, Shannon watched him descend. When one nail broke beneath his weight and clattered to the floor, he grunted, felt for another foothold and continued to climb down.

When he reached the ground, she said, "Wouldn't that be easier with a ladder?"

He shrugged. "If I had one, I would have used it."

Shannon noticed a large hammer and more of the big nails at her feet. He'd improvised. She liked that, but it seemed risky. He was here all alone. What if he'd fallen, been hurt? Days might have passed before help arrived. She gave herself a mental shake. No point in manufacturing worst-case scenarios. She needed to concentrate on the reason for her visit.

Smiling, she glanced into his face, finally able to see him clearly. His eyes were deep-set under thick brows and were an unusual light brown. The pupils were wide due to the dimness in the barn. When he looked at her, Shannon had the eerie feeling that he was looking right into her soul. Disconcerted, she quickly glanced at the rest of his face, the square jaw that had a small scar running diagonally across it, the fullness of his lips, which were at odds with the angled cheekbones, and a Roman nose, which had a slight bump in it as if it had been broken.

His face didn't match up to the rest of his body, but the physical imperfections only added character. This was a man who had worked hard, probably all his life, and expected to work hard for the rest of it, as well.

When his eyes met hers in a rapid, assessing glance, she experienced a moment of dizziness and placed her hand against the post he'd just descended.

"What do you want?" he repeated.

His impatient tone snapped her to the business at hand. Straightening, she indicated her clipboard. "I've been sent out to welcome you and let you know what services our natural resources agency can give to help you get the Crescent Ranch into shape.''

"No, thanks.'' He bent to pick up his tools.

Shannon gaped at him. "Excuse me?''

"I said no, thanks. I can handle it on my own.'' He nodded toward the door. "Close that behind you when you leave, would you?'' He turned to the tack room attached to the building.

It took her a few seconds to realize she'd been dismissed. She stared after him in stunned amazement, then she hurried behind him.

"I don't think you understand, Mr. Farraday,'' she insisted as she watched him put away tools and pick up a pair of gloves. "I'm here to help you. We would like you to participate in a project we're doing.''

He didn't even bother to turn around. "No, thanks. I don't have the time. I told that to the guy who called last week.''

"The guy who...'' Wiley, she thought, rocking to a stop. Irritation made her clench her fists at her sides. The same Wiley who had told her no one had contacted Luke. Well, it wasn't the first lie Wiley had told her.

Luke turned, and his gaze raked over her again. "Did they think that sending a beauty queen out would get me to change my mind?''

She stiffened. Sexism in the raw, she thought, infuriated. "I am a scientist, Mr. Farraday. I've worked in this field for three years now. I was born and raised in this county. Just on the other side of that mountain, in fact,'' she said, nodding toward Randall Peak. "I know what I'm doing. My looks have absolutely nothing to do with my abilities as a professional.''

He gave her a skeptical glance. "You've never used them to get what you want? Never batted those eyelashes of yours over those deep blue eyes?" His voice dropped to a gritty, intimate level that, to her horror, sent shivers up her spine. "Never used those full, sweet lips to whisper promises into eager ears? Promises you never intended to keep?"

"Certainly not!"

He snorted. "Right."

Appalled, Shannon stared at him. He was the most insulting, insufferable man she had ever met. She fought the urge to tell him so. Instead, she used her most clipped, professional voice as she said, "I'm sorry you can't get past my looks and accept me as a person who is here to help you. I would like to be able to take credit for my looks, but I can't. It's nothing I achieved on my own. I happen to come from a couple of good-looking parents," she informed him in a tight voice. Never mind that she didn't look very much like either one of them. They were both blondes.

Her father had said her long black hair, almond-shaped midnight blue eyes and high cheekbones were a throwback to her French great-grandmother. Her full lips had come straight from her mother.

"Whatever," he said, as if the subject bored him. "I'm not interested in participating in any study, or project, or anything else. I want to be left alone. I have a blocked stream I need to see to, so why don't you leave?"

He couldn't have made it any more clear, but Shannon wasn't going to give up. She had dealt with pigheaded men before, though not ones who had insulted and infuriated her on their first meeting.

She ignored his invitation to depart. Instead, she plastered a cool smile on her face and said, "Water problems happen to be my area of expertise, among others. Why don't I come along and help you solve it?"

"Because I don't want you, Miss, uh, Kipper."

"It's Kelleher," she corrected, speaking through her teeth. "Shannon Kelleher. Range conservation specialist." She withdrew her card from the little pocket attached to the front of her clipboard and handed it to him.

"Kelleher," he said quietly, as if he recognized her name. Reluctantly, he took the card she offered, his rough, callused fingers brushing hers as he did so. Shannon felt the warmth and texture of him, and for some reason, her eyes flew to his.

His gaze met hers with a steady assessment that she was startled to see was a little less disinterested than it had been a few minutes ago. For an instant, she thought he was seeing her as a person rather than a pretty face or an annoyance, but his eyelids flickered down, hiding his thoughts.

She couldn't have explained the intense disappointment she felt.

Luke tucked the card into his pocket. "Fine. If I ever need a range management specialist, Miss Kelleher, I'll be sure to call you," he said in a when-hell-freezes-over tone of voice.

"How do you know you don't need one now?" He started from the barn and she stalked after him.

"I've been ranching since before you were born. I don't need you to tell me how to do it."

Shannon seriously doubted the first part of that statement. In spite of his weathered skin and the lines that rayed out from the corners of his eyes, he didn't appear to be much more than five years past her own twenty-seven. In the strong sunlight of the barnyard, she could see that his hair was a deep, rich brown, almost as dark as hers. It was thick, in need of a trim but untouched by gray. He ran his hand through it and settled his hat on his head.

"I'm not here to tell you how to ranch, but am I right in assuming you're new to southern Colorado?"

He looked at her for a second as if weighing her question for hidden traps, then he nodded. "That's right. I'm from Arizona. Near Tucson."

She opened her hands wide. "There you go, then. We have different terrain, different climate, different plants, different water problems. I can help you learn about all of those things."

He shook his head. "You're as persistent as fleas on a dog's belly, aren't you?"

Shannon tucked her chin in and lifted her eyes to him ruefully. "Well, I've never heard it put quite that way, but I guess so."

As they had been walking across the barnyard, he had been slapping his gloves across his palm. Now he tucked them into his waistband as he reached to untie a big roan gelding tethered to the corral fence. "Since it doesn't look like I'm going to get rid of you, you can tag along." He swung into the saddle. "But you'll have to catch and saddle your own mount." He gathered the reins and headed the gelding out of the yard.

"Aren't you going to wait..." she asked, then realized she was talking to the air. He spurred his horse with his heels and galloped away.

She slapped her clipboard against her thigh. "Of all the..." He thought she wouldn't catch and saddle her own mount, she thought furiously. He thought she *couldn't*.

The light of challenge sparked in Shannon's eyes. Little did he know. She watched to see which direction he had taken, then she whirled and raced to the tack room. She was dressed for riding in the clothes she usually wore to work, jeans, soft and snug from many wearings and washings, a long-sleeved shirt of pale yellow cotton, her sturdy boots and a woman's cowboy hat. Nothing was going to stop her from following him.

In the tack room, she picked out a saddle blanket and a saddle and bridle, hoisted them onto her shoulder and started for the corral.

The swiftness of her movements made her head spin, and she had to stop for a second and catch her breath when dizziness swirled through her. Cursing the lingering infection that was still slowing her down, she picked out a nondescript brown mare with a wide chest and powerful legs. Bridle in hand, she eased into the corral and moved slowly and steadily forward. She spoke in the soft, quietly crooning tone her father had taught her and cornered the animal quickly.

She slipped the bit into the mare's mouth, complimenting her on what a well-mannered young lady she was. "Unlike your owner," Shannon muttered to the horse. "What is that man's problem, anyway?"

The horse tossed her head as if to say she didn't know, either, and Shannon laughed. Within a few minutes, she was mounted and heading across the fields after her reluctant host. She concentrated on the ride and quickly caught onto the mare's smooth gait. Shannon was pleased with her choice. The horse's easy stride didn't jostle her head, which would have increased her dizziness. Leaning over the mare's head, she urged her into a run.

It wasn't long before she found Luke at the stream where it crossed over from his neighbor's spread. It was a pretty spot, with a small line cabin nearby. Luke stood with his mount's reins in his hand as he gazed across the fence.

He didn't even turn when Shannon approached. She dismounted and led the mare to stand beside him. It wasn't necessary to ask what the problem was, she could see it for herself.

They'd had a heavy rain the week before, along with lightning. A bolt must have hit a cottonwood tree that stood on the bank of the creek. It had been blasted in half. Branches had fallen into the creek, blocking the narrow channel. Water spread over the land, much of it evaporating in the heat before it could trickle into the path that fed water into Luke's pond.

"That's easy to fix," Shannon said.

Luke glanced at her. "I have to wonder why it hasn't been fixed before. Do you think my neighbor was hoping to keep all the water for himself?"

Yet again, Shannon stared at him. It was gradually

dawning on her that this man's rudeness to her wasn't personal. He didn't seem to like anybody.

"Your neighbor is Violet Beardsley. She's a nice lady, a good neighbor. If she'd known about this blockage, she would have cleared it." Shannon placed her foot on the bottom strand of barbed wire and grabbed the second strand, stretching a gap in the fence. "We can go through and clear it now. She won't mind at all."

Luke lifted a skeptical brow at her. "I have your word on that?"

"Certainly!"

He reached to hold the barbed wire. "Ladies first, then."

His direct, challenging gaze made her wonder if he thought she was afraid to get dirty. Shannon took off her hat and tossed it lightly over the fence, where it landed rakishly on a sagebrush.

When she paused before ducking under the wire and looked at him, his hard mouth smiled grimly. "Don't worry. I won't let it go."

Embarrassed because that was exactly what she had been thinking, Shannon crouched and scrambled through. She turned to hold the wire for him, then scooped up her hat and clapped it onto her head.

Luke walked to the stream and began wrestling the branch out of the way. Shannon hurried to help him, grabbing a branch and dragging it. Seeing the expression in his eyes made Shannon repeat to herself the question she'd asked the mare a little while before. What *was* this man's problem?

She hoped her help would convince him of her good intentions, but she had to stop a couple of times and catch her breath when she bent over too quickly and her head spun. She hid it, though, not willing to let Luke see her showing weakness. Surreptitiously, she filled her cupped hands with some of the cool stream water and splashed it on her face to revive herself.

When they were finished and the water was once more flowing in its natural channel, they returned to Luke's side of the fence.

Shannon immediately launched into a speech about the water table and the changes that had developed in the area over the years in the plants and grasses that grew on his ranch, about how last week's rain had run off rather than soaked in.

Luke interrupted her. "That's just fine, Miss Kelleher, but you're wasting your breath. I—" He stopped and his eyes sharpened as if he'd just experienced a mental finger snap. "Kelleher. Now I remember. Gus Blackhawk said your family was the one that tried to buy this place, but he wouldn't sell to you."

"It wasn't my family," she said quickly. "It was two of my cousins, Ben and Tim Sills."

"Blackhawk said none of you were too happy that he sold to me instead."

"Mr. Blackhawk was exaggerating," Shannon said, giving him a steady look. Ben and Tim had wanted the ranch badly. They'd pooled their money and borrowed from friends and family, but they'd come short of the asking price.

"So your visit here today has nothing to do with wanting to check out the man who bought this place from under your cousins' noses? You're not interested in trying to find out if I'll turn right around and sell to them?''

''I'm here in my strictly professional capacity,'' she answered tightly. ''I already know some of the situation on this ranch. I can help. There are government grants available to you to help solve your water and grass problem.''

Luke's jaw tightened. He leaned close, speaking slowly and clearly as if to insure there would be no misunderstanding. ''Government money comes with government strings, Miss Kelleher, and no one is going to tell me how to run my ranch.''

She'd met this attitude before, but never quite so vehemently. She took a breath and tried to quell the anger that was simmering inside her. ''I'm not, but there's a unique opportunity here to do some good, to bring this place back to it's natural state—''

''Which would probably be impossible with you government types stomping all over, sticking your noses into my business.''

''That's not true. We only want to help.''

He stuck his face close to hers. ''I've been on the receiving end of that kind of *help* before. I want no part of it.''

''You're being completely unreasonable.'' Frustrated, Shannon turned and gazed over his pasture. Her head spun again, and she widened her stance to maintain her balance. She closed her eyes for a moment until her head cleared.

Luke's sharp gaze didn't miss her moment of weakness. His hand shot out to grasp her shoulder. ''Is something wrong with you?''

''No,'' she said testily, startled by his touch. ''I'm

fine.'' She shrugged off his hand because it seemed to weigh as heavily as an anvil on her. She forced the dizziness back, and when it settled, she pointed across the field. "Look at that grass."

"There's plenty of it."

"It's brown and dry. No nutrition in it at all."

"I can see that, but I have other fields."

"How many cattle are you planning to run?"

"Not that it's any of your business," he answered in a harsh tone. "But I'll probably start out with five hundred head."

"Your other fields probably can't support that. They're not in much better shape than this one. This field was badly overgrazed by your good friend Gus Blackhawk," she said, then could have bitten her tongue at the sharp words. She took a breath, lifted her chin and met his gaze. He was glaring at her. "It's been standing idle for years, but the grass hasn't come back. The deer and elk won't even touch it. It needs serious, concentrated intervention to bring it back."

"Which I can do on my own," he insisted. "I told you already that I don't need your help. What's the point of owning a huge spread like this, having all this to run, to own, if I'm going to let you or anyone else come in and tell me what to do?"

His tone blew all her good intentions to the four winds. Shannon clapped her hands onto her hips. "You're being impossibly stubborn! Take a look at this." She bent to grab a handful of the dry grass to show him what she meant. She moved too quickly, though. Before she could prevent it, dizziness swirled through her, followed by blackness. With a soft groan, she folded up right at Luke Farraday's boot tips.

CHAPTER TWO

"I HAVE to tell you, lady, this is a day for firsts. My first female scientist giving me my first lessons on how to run my place and the first time I've ever had a beautiful woman faint at my feet. If you welcome everyone to Tarrant County this way, it's a wonder there's been any growth in the population here at all."

Shannon could barely hear Luke's voice. It seemed to be coming from miles away. She knew she should have been able to hear him more clearly. After all, her head was against his chest as he carried her with one arm under her knees, the other across her back. She was not a small woman, but he had picked her up as if she weighed no more than a feather pillow.

Her head lolled, seeming to have found its own special resting place between his jaw and his collarbone. As tough as this man was, it should have felt like having her head caught in a vise. Instead, it felt snug, warm and welcoming. For a crazy instant, she fantasized that it was a spot fashioned especially for her. She knew the idea was outlandish and that as soon as she felt better, her sanity would return, but right now, she didn't mind indulging in the fantasy—and in the comfort he offered.

Giddily, she decided that the best thing about being carried by him was the way he smelled, spicy, faintly sweaty yet all male. Not that she should even be noticing such things, what with her head still spinning, but somehow it soothed her. Her stomach had settled a bit, but she would be grateful to get out of the sun.

Seeming to read her mind, Luke carried her to someplace cool and dark. Shannon opened her eyes to see that he had brought her into the old line cabin she'd seen earlier. She noticed that it was a charming little place, built of sturdy timber, not the ramshackle shack she'd thought it to be. There was a wood-burning stove in one corner and two shuttered windows that could provide cross ventilation. There were two cots with rolled-up mattresses.

"You can lie down here for a minute," Luke said as he stopped and set her on her feet. He wrapped one arm around her and leaned her against him as he unrolled one of the mattresses, then eased her down on it.

Before she could say anything, he turned and left. Shannon blinked at the ceiling as she wondered where he'd disappeared to. He came back a few minutes later carrying a canteen.

She reached for it, but he gave her a look and sat beside her. "I'll hold it," he said, slipping one arm under her to lift her as he held the canteen to her lips. His touch continued to be gentle, filling her with tenderness she couldn't quite understand. As she drank, she looked in confusion to study his expression. His jaw was set as firmly as a bear trap, his eyes shadowed, but he treated her as carefully as he would a small child. Confused, she paused after one swallow.

He looked at her, his brows drawing together in a frown. "More," he said in a gruff tone. "If you didn't feel well, you shouldn't have started out today with no water."

"I have some...in the truck," she said, dutifully drinking more water as he pressed the metal opening to her lips.

He grunted as if asking why she hadn't brought it along with her to the creek. Given his bluntness, she didn't know why he didn't voice the question. When she was finished, he settled her onto the mattress, then stunned her by removing a clean handkerchief from his pocket, wetting it and bathing her face.

Casually, he reached for the buttons on her blouse.

Her hand fluttered up to stop him. "No," she gasped. This was getting way more personal than she wanted it to be.

He raised one of his thick, dark brows. "I'm not planning to try anything. Women who faint at my feet don't turn me on."

"How do you know?" she asked. "You said I'm the first one who's ever done it." Heat rushed into her face, and she wished she could call the words back.

She saw humor spark in those unusual caramel-colored eyes of his. "I only had to be kicked in the head by a horse once to know I didn't like it."

Whatever that meant, she thought, disgruntled as he casually unbuttoned the first three buttons of her blouse and bathed her throat and chest. His touch may have been disinterested, but her reaction wasn't. Her heart kicked into quick time, and she was sure he could see it pounding in her throat, feel it as he swabbed the area above the swell of her breasts—which was instantly bathed in a rush of heat. She was surprised steam didn't rise from her skin.

"Th-thank you," she stammered, rounding her

shoulders to discourage his touch, though to her shame, her treacherous body liked it too much. "I feel better now."

Luke's answer was a nod of acknowledgment as he stood. He watched her shaky fingers do up her buttons, then he crossed the room, tossed the damp handkerchief on a small wooden table, pulled a chair out and carried it across to her. Spinning it so the back faced her, he straddled it and placed his arms along the top. His gaze swept her again, sending a tingle of awareness through her.

Shannon's eyes skittered away from his. She wished from the depth of her soul that she could get up and get out of here, but whenever she tried to lift her head, the world tilted on its axis. She didn't like being at a disadvantage, and with Luke Farraday, it seemed even worse than it would have been with anyone else.

After a minute, he asked, "Are you pregnant?"

Her startled gaze flew to meet his. His eyes met hers with a cynical expression. "Certainly not," she sputtered. "I'm not even married!"

That brought a rusty laugh from him. It sounded as if he hadn't used it in a while. "Miss Kelleher, I think we both know marriage isn't required to produce a baby."

"I'm not pregnant," she said quietly but firmly. "I've been sick with an ear infection. It's better, but…"

"But you should have stayed home in bed until you were well. Why didn't you?"

She was stunned that he seemed to be angry with her. After all, no one had forced him to help her. He could have left her crumpled on the ground to recover on her own. "I had to get back to work. My boss..." She realized that her boss had wanted her to come to work today in order to deal with the man in front of her. Good old Wiley, she thought. His philosophy was, Why deal with a problem if you can get someone else do it?

She wasn't going to tell Luke that. She'd already blown her professional image. No point in telling him of her problems with Wiley—no matter how numerous they were.

"Your boss insisted you come to work? Why didn't you stand up to him?" Luke asked, irritation simmering in his voice. "You don't have any trouble standing up to me."

"You're not in charge of my biannual performance review," she answered ruefully. "Or my salary raises."

"Maybe you should talk to the person in charge of *his*," Luke suggested.

"I might if his boss wasn't also his mother's brother."

"Ah." Luke tilted his head back. "Nepotism lives."

"I'm afraid so," Shannon agreed weakly. She wished she hadn't said that, but she couldn't call it back. She seemed to be making one stumbling, bumbling mistake after another today. Luke was right. She should have stayed home until she was well. She was here now, so she was determined to struggle through.

"Mr. Farraday," she said, trying to sound briskly competent in spite of the weakness in her voice. "Thank you for helping me." She sat up shakily and swung her feet to the floor. To her intense relief, the world remained firm and didn't do one of those nauseating spins she'd been experiencing all day. She was pleased that she felt only a slight tremor in her hand when she smoothed her hair from her face. She took a steadying breath and glanced at him. "Now, why don't we return to our discussion about your rangeland?"

"Because the discussion is closed," he answered, standing and returning the chair to its place. He stood with his hands resting on his hips while his eyes narrowly assessed the color in her cheeks. "If you're feeling better, let's get you back to your truck. It's time for you to go."

Shannon gaped at him. "Really, Mr. Farraday, you can't just refuse our help—"

"Of course I can. Haven't you heard? It's a free country. This is my place, and I'm my own boss." In spite of his dismissive words, he hovered over her as she stood shakily, then took her arm and helped her to the door, gathering his canteen and handkerchief along the way.

She wanted to argue, but she didn't have the strength. He led her to the gelding he'd ridden to the stream. "We'll ride double on Dusty," he said. "I don't want you falling off of Jezebel."

Shannon laughed. "That gentle animal's name is Jezebel?"

He shrugged, and again she saw that spark of humor. "How was I to know when she was a filly that she'd turn out to be such a lady?"

Shannon grabbed the pommel and placed her left

foot in the stirrup as she looked over her shoulder at him. "You sound surprised."

He stood behind her and placed his hands at her waist. "Not surprised. Wary." With what seemed like the smallest flexing of his muscles, he boosted her into the saddle. "I've learned that wariness pays when dealing with the female of any species," he said, turning to snag Jezebel's reins and scooping Shannon's hat from the ground.

Dazed, Shannon replaced her hat while she settled into the saddle. She kept her feet out of the stirrups so that Luke could mount. She wasn't prepared for her reaction when he did. Awareness moved along her nerves like an incoming tide, first along the backs of her legs where they touched his, then her back, and finally up her spine, across her shoulders and down her arms as he reached forward, tied Jezebel's reins to the pommel, then gathered those of his own horse. He clucked to Dusty and turned toward the ranch buildings.

Shannon, accustomed to handling her own mount, didn't know quite what to do with her hands as they rode along. She refused to hold on to the pommel like a tenderfoot, so she tightened her knees against the mare's sides to hold herself steady and settled her hands on her thighs. Glancing down, she saw that if she moved her hands back a few inches, she could touch Luke. Unexpectedly, her palms grew warm at the thought, and it made her even more light-headed than she'd been when she fainted.

She didn't know what was wrong with her. These strange reactions couldn't be attributed to her illness. Something about Luke Farraday was affecting her in the oddest way. Was it because he was a stranger? Most of the ranchers and farmers she dealt with were people she'd known all her life. Maybe it was because he seemed so distant and unyielding. Whatever the reason, she needed to get her mind on business.

Grimly, she straightened away from Luke. "This is a wonderful ranch you've bought here," she ventured.

"Even if the grass won't support five hundred head of cattle?" he asked in a dry tone.

His deep voice vibrated through her, distracting her from her purpose. Strangely, she felt as if the timbre and vibration of his voice set off an answering chord in her. She leaned forward to escape that sensation. "With some work and proper management, we could have it in shape in no time."

"I'll do it myself."

"So you said." Shannon twisted to look at him. Their eyes met, and she was temporarily distracted when she noticed that his eyes had flecks of gold in them, which only added to their unique appearance. She forced her mind on track. "I'm sure you'll try to do what you can here, but you need an expert. You need me."

He set his jaw, and his eyes raked over her. "I have to wonder why this is so important to you."

"It's my job."

"Is that all? Or could it be because it'll enhance your reputation if you can do what that guy who called last week couldn't do?"

Stung partly because it was true, she turned. "Of course not."

He gave another one of those dry laughs. "Can it, Miss Kelleher. I've already said no."

Shannon's mouth tightened. "I heard you."

"But you don't listen very well."

She ignored that. "Do you know the history of this ranch?"

"As much as I need to know."

His tone discouraged discussion, but she forged ahead anyway. She could be stubborn, too. "The Crescent Ranch is one of the last intact spreads in this area. It was homesteaded at the turn of the century by the Crescent family. The last member, Millard, built the fancy rock ranch house but should have put some of that money back into range management and improvement. He didn't, though, and lost the place during the Depression. It's had half a dozen different owners since then, until Gus Blackhawk bought it about thirty years ago. Some people say he bought it for his son, Garrett, but Garrett didn't want it, so it's been leased since then. I guess old Gus thought his son would change his mind someday and come back to live here."

"Thanks for the update on local gossip," Luke said.

"Sorry," she answered, miffed. "I just thought you'd be interested in the past so you'd know what to avoid in the future."

"I already know what to avoid. Interference."

"So you said."

"Just keep in mind how impossibly stubborn I am."

She winced at having her words thrown back at her. "I shouldn't have said that. I apologize."

"Why apologize?" he asked with a shrug. "It's the truth."

Shannon gave up and made no further attempts at conversation as they rode across the range. Looking around, she felt sad at the knowledge that this ranch would never be returned to the lush vegetation it had once known.

When they reached the barn, Luke dismounted and helped her down. "Are you all right to drive back to town?"

"Yes." She was worn-out, but she couldn't admit it. Maybe her time with him had made her as stubborn as he was.

As if he didn't believe her, Luke grasped her chin. Tilting her head, he looked into her eyes as if checking her pupils. Shannon's gaze flew to meet his. "I'm fine," she said.

Luke didn't release her jaw. Instead his touch lingered. His eyes studied her face. One corner of his mouth tilted upward, but it wasn't a smile. "Beautiful," he said, his voice rough. "You're too damned beautiful."

The way he said it was an insult. Shannon snapped her head out of his grasp and nearly sent herself into another swoon. She turned, plucked the keys from her pocket and scrabbled for the truck's door handle. He was there ahead of her.

"You're in no shape to do this." He rapped the words out. "I'll drive you back to town."

"Absolutely not," she responded, her eyes flashing as she turned to him. "You've done quite enough."

"No, I haven't." He snagged the keys from her hand. "I'll be right back."

Shannon watched in impotent fury as he took the horses to the barn, unsaddled them and turned them into the corral. She wanted to run after him and demand the return of the keys. Unfortunately, he was right. She was in no shape to drive or to go tearing around after him.

But he didn't have to be so high-handed about it.

Accepting defeat, she climbed into the truck and sat behind the wheel, arms folded and lips drawn into an angry line as she waited for him to return with the keys. He was back within a few minutes and didn't even pause when he saw her. He scooted her aside and took her place behind the steering wheel.

"I guess it won't do any good to point out that this vehicle belongs to the agency and only its employees are allowed to drive it?" she asked.

"You're right. It won't do any good at all. Fasten your seat belt."

"How will you get home?"

Luke stuck his right thumb in the air. "I'll hitch-hike."

Shannon turned in her seat to examine his grim profile, the hard set of his jaw. With his face shadowed beneath the brim of his black hat, he reminded her of a gunslinger of the old west. "Oh, yeah," she said. "There'll be any number of people willing to pick *you* up."

"I bet you'd be surprised."

"Not today," she said wearily. "Nothing about you would surprise me."

He stopped at the highway to wait for traffic and shaved a look in her direction. "You don't have this whole diplomacy thing down too firmly, do you, Miss Kelleher?''

"I thought I did until I met you, *Mr.* Farraday."

That brought another of those gritty laughs.

Shannon didn't respond. She wasn't accustomed to feeling unsettled, infuriated and powerless all at the same time. She'd never been around any man who was so determined to have his own way, who was so convinced his own way was right.

Turning her head, she stared at the scenery they passed. Cattle grazing in the lush grass in a field belonging to the McAdam family gave way to a field of prairie flax waving its lavender blossoms in the breeze. Two years ago, their fields had been as badly overgrazed as Luke's, but they'd prospered with a little help from her and lots of good management by the McAdams. She wouldn't waste her breath telling Luke that, though.

She told herself it was none of her business. She had tried and failed, but it galled her.

"Sulking won't make me change my mind," Luke said, giving her a sideways glance.

She crossed her arms over her chest.

"You could also stick your bottom lip out and start crying, but that won't make me change my mind, either."

Chin in the air, she said, "Even if I thought it would, I wouldn't resort to that. I'm a professional."

He didn't answer, but she saw his face twitch. If she didn't know better, she would have thought he was fighting a grin.

They reached Tarrant within twenty minutes, and she directed him to the agency's office building. It was a small redbrick structure, and the windows of Wiley's office faced the parking lot. Shannon noticed a shadow behind the miniblinds and knew that her boss lurked there, watching her arrival. He would have something to say to her about letting Luke drive her back to the office. That was okay, though. She had plenty to say to him.

Luke parked the truck, stepped out and hurried around to help her out before she could gather her clipboard and reach for the door handle. When she opened her mouth to speak, he held up his hand. "Don't bother to thank me. I know you wouldn't mean it."

"No," she responded, exasperated. "I wouldn't."

His long, callused fingers touched the brim of his hat. "Then let's don't be hypocritical by wishing each other a good day. It hasn't been a good day for either of us." With that, he turned and strode toward the street, his long legs and easy stride covering the distance in seconds.

Watching him go, Shannon slumped against the side of the truck and shook her head. "Who was that masked man?" she whispered with a silent laugh. She felt as if she'd spent three hours in his company and knew little more than she had when she'd stood on the floor of his barn and appreciated the sight of his backside.

In that time, she had gone through almost every emotion a person could feel, from appreciation to happiness to fury and indignation. No wonder she was dizzy.

Luke strode around the corner, then stopped and stepped back to see if Shannon was all right. She was just disappearing inside the building. Good. She was safely in her office, at her job, in her own life. She wouldn't be coming to his place again. He'd made sure of that, though he knew he should be ashamed of his rudeness.

He resumed walking down the wide sidewalk of Tarrant's main street. If he'd been capable of it, he would have stopped to appreciate what a pretty little town it was, but he hadn't chosen the area for the beauty of its county seat. He'd bought the Crescent Ranch because he could afford it and he could own it outright. No sharing. Never again would he be in a position to let someone have a say in his place. Not financially. Not agriculturally.

Not even a beautiful range management specialist with midnight blue eyes and black hair was going to tell him how to run his place. Unconsciously, Luke's hand went to the pocket where he'd tucked her card. Yeah, he'd kept it, though he didn't know why. He'd never use it.

What he had told her was true. She was too damned beautiful. She was also too damned disturbing. He didn't need that. He had work to do. Alone. He liked it that way.

He crossed to the side of the street where the traffic was heading east, toward home, and stuck out his thumb. The irony of thinking such thoughts, then begging for a ride wasn't lost on him, but he wasn't going to make a practice of asking for things from his neighbors, not even rides. The fewer things he asked for, the fewer obligations he had, the less he would be disappointed. Hurt.

It didn't take a genius to figure out that there was something in Shannon Kelleher's big eyes and sweet mouth that could disappoint and hurt a man. He didn't need that.

But her card was in his pocket, and he left it there.

Wiley pounced as soon as she walked in the door. "Who was that guy? And what was he doing driving my truck?"

Shannon lifted an eyebrow as she skirted around him and headed for her small office. "When did the agency sign the truck over to be your personal vehicle?"

"You know what I mean." He dogged her steps.

In a cool tone, Shannon explained what had happened. Typically, Wiley didn't express any concern for her welfare. She wasn't surprised. Her boss was a secretive man whose main interest was himself.

"I know you lied to me when you said no one had contacted him." She pointed a finger at him. "*You* tried to call him on the phone last week, and when he wouldn't talk to you, you sent me out there. How I got back is my own business."

Wiley's ferocious frown told her he didn't care that she knew he'd lied. "Did you do any good out there? Get him to sign on for the project?"

Shannon locked her shoulder bag in her desk drawer and sat down to go through her mail. "Not yet. But I will." She wished she felt the confidence she put into her voice.

"Humph," he said, turning to leave her office. "You can't do this job. They should have hired a man for it."

Shannon wanted to respond that they should have hired a man for Wiley's job, too, but that would surely get her into hot water. She was growing weary of the constant struggles with him, and lately his animosity was tinged with an undercurrent she couldn't quite put her finger on. He watched everything she did almost jealously, but she concluded it was because he had wanted his nephew to get her job. She could only think that he couldn't seem to forgive her for being better qualified for the job—or for being a woman. Her only consolation was the knowledge that it was his problem, not hers.

As she cleared her desk, Shannon came across the paperwork she'd begun to get Ben and Timmy started on the lengthy grant awards process. They would have needed government money to fix up the Crescent Ranch. Except for their names and the date of purchase, she had filled in all the necessary information. It was true that she wanted to help her cousins, but it was part of her job. She would have done the same thing for a total stranger like Luke Farraday. Maybe she still could. She would hold on to these. He might change his mind. With a wry smile, Shannon told herself she was being ridiculously optimistic. She dropped the forms into a drawer and closed it.

She propped her elbows on her desk and pressed her fingertips to her lips as she wondered if there was any way to get him to change his mind. He'd told her that he didn't want anyone telling him how to run his place, but she thought there was more to it than that. She didn't know any rancher who liked government interference, but most of them were willing to work with her for the betterment of their land and cattle.

She would have to think about the situation with Luke and see if she could come up with a better approach—just as soon as she stopped dwelling on what a disturbingly attractive man he was.

On Saturday morning, Shannon happily snuggled her two-month-old niece, Christina, against her chest and tucked a light blanket around her as they made their way down the sidewalk of Tarrant's business district. Her mother and two sisters, Brittnie and Becca, were at the grand opening of Lauren's Boutique, a shop owned by a friend of the family. Shannon, who hated shopping on the best of days, had no desire to go into that crowd no matter how much she wished Lauren well, so she had volunteered to take care of Becca's baby.

Her family teased that she really didn't care very much about clothes, and that was true, though she'd sought to please them today by dressing in a red shorts and top outfit that Brittnie had brought back last November from her honeymoon in Mexico. She liked the outfit because the shorts weren't too snug or revealing and the top was loose enough to be comfortable.

Shannon pushed the stroller with one hand, held the baby with the other and drifted down the walk, gazing in windows and stopping frequently to talk to shoppers, most of them friends who wanted a look at Christina.

The sidewalk ended in front of the feed store, and she started to turn toward the boutique only to get the stroller caught in a crack in the sidewalk. Carefully supporting Christina, she was bending to free it when a hand came down, picked the stroller up and spun it around in the direction she wanted to go.

"Thanks," she said, smiling and glancing up. She straightened abruptly, and surprise sponged the smile off her lips when she saw that her rescuer was Luke Farraday. "Oh, it's you."

He lifted a brow at her. "So it seems. Are you feeling better?"

The solicitous words were belied by the coolness of his tone. Shannon wondered why the contrasts in this man seemed to fascinate her so much. It had been more than a week since she'd been to his ranch, but she'd thought about him every day. "Yes," she finally said. "I'm completely well now."

He nodded toward Christina. "Not yours, I take it, since you told me you're not married."

"My niece." Shannon turned Christina so Luke could see her face. The whole Kelleher Saunders family agreed that she was an exceptionally beautiful baby, with her dark eyes and wispy hair. The baby looked at Luke and broke into one of her rare smiles.

Shannon glanced up in time to see something move in Luke's eyes, a swift shadow of longing that first set her back on her heels, then made her doubt what she had seen, so quickly was it gone.

The thought flashed through her mind that he was determined to remain a loner, but even he had vulnerabilities. She wondered if it could be that he had the same needs most people had for family. She wished she knew more about him. She knew he lived, and ranched, alone.

Luke's gaze flashed to hers, and the softness she'd seen disappeared. She glanced down to see he was carrying a box of items from the feed store. "You've been shopping," she said lamely.

"Isn't that what everyone's doing here on a Saturday morning?" he asked, nodding toward the mass of shoppers. "Except you, it seems."

"I only shop when my back's to the wall."

"You don't like buying stacks of new clothes, maybe some diamonds, a fur coat?"

She burst out laughing. "And wear them where? To help Pete Minton reseed his north pasture? Luke, you're a riot."

At her flippant tone, he narrowed his eyes. "Then you're an unusual woman."

"I thought we'd already established that."

"Yeah, I guess we did." He tipped his hat to her and started to turn away, but he paused, looking up the sidewalk with a frown.

CHAPTER THREE

SHANNON'S attention followed his to see what he was looking at. Automatically, she stiffened at the sight of Gus Blackhawk approaching. His feet shuffled as if he could barely lift them. His gray hair was disheveled, as were his clothes. He wore jeans and a faded green shirt topped by a winter jacket, despite the heat of the June day.

Shannon gaped at him. She hadn't seen him in months and had never seen him looking like this. He was a proud man, always well-dressed, disdainful of those he considered beneath him. But today he looked like a bum. Even as her heart went out to him, she tightened her arms protectively around Christina.

Luke saw her movement and gave her a curious look just as Mr. Blackhawk reached them. He would have passed them by, but Luke said, "Good morning, Mr. Blackhawk," and the old man stopped.

His eyes, once a deep, dark blue, now murky, lifted to Luke. He stared for a few seconds before he responded, "Oh, Farraday. Yeah, hello." Unfocused, his gaze slanted to Shannon and Christina. He studied her blankly for a moment, then his lip curled. "You're that girl of Mary Jane's. Bet your family wasn't too happy when I sold to this guy, huh?"

Shannon was offended by his gloating tone, but before she could react, Luke gave her a swift glance and broke in. "Mr. Blackhawk," he said. "We're sorry we interrupted your...business." He stunned Shannon by stepping protectively between her and the old man. His voice was harder than steel as he said, "We'll let you be on your way."

Mr. Blackhawk blinked as if he'd forgotten Luke was there and couldn't understand why he was interfering. Shannon swallowed a bubble of hysteria. She couldn't understand it, either, but she was grateful.

Luke shifted the box he carried to his hip, then he took Shannon's arm and turned her, stroller and all, hustling her and her niece down the sidewalk.

Shannon stumbled along with him, upset and disconcerted. "Thank you," she stammered. "I wish I could tell you what that was all about. He's an unhappy old man who's always disliked my family, but—"

Luke sliced a glance at her, his jaw set, his eyes cold. "It's his problem, not yours."

"I guess so." She was taken aback by Luke's swift protectiveness. She knew it was old-fashioned chivalry and nothing personal, but still, she was speechless with surprise. When they arrived in front of Lauren's Boutique, she stopped him. "I'm meeting my family here." She sent him a grateful smile. "Thank you again. You were very considerate and...chivalrous in the face of his rudeness." She blushed. Luke had been rude to her the day they had met.

Strangely, he didn't seem to welcome her gratitude. Maybe he, too, was recalling his rudeness. "I'll be going then," he said. "Goodbye, Miss Kelleher."

Shannon hugged her niece and swayed as she watched him turn swiftly and stroll away. She was grateful to see that Gus Blackhawk was nowhere in sight. Luke reached a brown pickup, set the box in the back and climbed in, then reversed out of the spot and drove down the street.

Shannon saw that his truck still had its Arizona license plate. His vehicle told her a little bit more about him. He might have the money to buy the Crescent Ranch and to take his time about getting it into shape to raise cattle, but he didn't waste his funds on a new truck when a ten-year old one would get him where he needed to go.

This was becoming like a game, she thought, as she bent to place Christina in her stroller and strap her in carefully. The more she wanted to learn about Luke Farraday, the more he seemed to hide. That was why he fascinated her. She was convinced that once she got to know him, he wouldn't seem so intriguing.

Shannon had always liked puzzles and ciphers, and Luke certainly qualified. The way to solve a puzzle was to find its secret key.

Shannon gave Luke a week after seeing him in Tarrant. He hadn't contacted her office—not that she thought he would. He'd made it clear that he didn't want help from her or any other person or agency. Ordinarily, she would respect that, but she was sure that, given a little more time and persuasion, she could get him to change his mind.

Her motives weren't purely unselfish, she admitted, as she packed a lunch to take on Friday's rounds. While it was true that thinking about the methods she could use to get the Crescent back into shape was enough to make her excited about the project, she also wanted to prove to Wiley Frost that she could do her job.

She leaned against the kitchen counter to sip her morning coffee. Absently, her gaze scanned her apartment. Though it was tiny and furnished with castoffs from the homes of her mother and sisters, it was cheerful and full of the shades of blue and green she loved. Plants flourished before the big window that looked on the small apartment building's lawn. She moved from the kitchen area and examined the plants, plucking a few dry leaves off the philodendron.

Her problems with Wiley were only part of the reason she needed to talk to Luke again. There was something about Luke that intrigued her, drew her to him. Maybe it was because he seemed like such a loner, though she was sure he would deny being lonely. Maybe it was because he didn't seem to like her.

While she didn't feel any particular need to be liked by everyone she met, she thrived on challenge. Her mother said she'd always done things the hard way, and Shannon knew she probably wasn't going to change. And dealing with Luke was definitely a challenge.

With a determined step, she returned to the kitchen, set her cup down and finished making her salad. As she was reaching for some cookies to add to her lunch, she paused and tilted her head. She and her nephew, Jimmy, had made the chocolate chip cookies last night when he'd come to spend the evening with her. Even though his help had consisted of scooping out and eating chunks of dough when he thought she wasn't looking, the cookies had turned out to be delicious.

Shannon examined the container with narrowed eyes, then smiled ruefully. Luke Farraday definitely didn't seem like the type of man who would be influenced by baked goods. She was sure that the way to his heart was *not* through his stomach, but still, cookies might soften him up.

Unbelievable that she was thinking in these terms. She'd spent her life trying to be accepted for her brains rather than her looks or her abilities in the kitchen. The idea of being seen as a helpless female was abhorrent to her though she was also practical enough to know that she'd damaged her image when she'd fainted at Luke's feet.

Smiling, she gathered a handful of cookies and tossed them into a self-sealing bag. The truth was, she was a fabulous cook, and there was the barest outside chance that taking him a few cookies might make him pause long enough to get him to listen to her. She had two other ranches to visit first. Then she would spend the rest of the day with Luke.

If he would let her.

"This better be a neighborly visit and not an official one," Luke said as he strode toward where she'd parked the agency truck.

When she had driven into the yard, she'd seen him coming out of the barn with a roll of barbed wire, which he'd tossed into the back of his truck. She was relieved that she'd caught him. If she'd been a few minutes later, he would have been gone.

Seeing him striding toward her in his work clothes

of denim shirt, jeans and dusty boots, his accustomed scowl fixed in its usual place just under the brim of his battered straw cowboy hat, she felt a surge of excitement and anticipation. Since meeting him, she'd somehow become enthralled with the idea of living dangerously.

Shannon grabbed the bag of cookies and let it dangle from her fingers as she stepped to the ground. When she answered him, her tone was as direct as his. "Oh? You're accepting neighborly visits, then?"

Luke stopped in front of her and rested his hands on his waist as his gaze shifted from her to the bag and back again. "That depends. Are you the local welcoming committee today?"

"No, just one neighbor calling on another."

Luke stripped his gloves off and stuck them in his back pocket, then took the bag and extracted a couple of cookies. As he did so, he gave her an assessing glance. "What else do neighbors do to help each other out around here?"

She knew intuitively that he was testing her. She lifted her chin. "Whatever needs to be done. Last year, Joe McAdam helped my mom load and sell some cattle after she fell and hurt her back." Shannon smiled ruefully. "My mom's a little bit accident prone." She didn't know why she'd added the last part, except it wouldn't hurt for him to begin seeing his neighbors as real people.

He bit into a cookie and chewed it thoughtfully, then held it away and gave it an appreciative look. "You make these?"

"Yes. With my nephew's help."

He took another bite, chewed and swallowed. "Had any experience in mending fences?"

Shannon blinked. "Are you kidding? I'm one of three girls. We had no brothers, so our dad depended on us to help out." She offered him a tentative smile. "You got some fence that needs mending?"

His gaze went from her to cookies and back again. "Can you mend fence as well as you bake cookies?"

"Better."

As she had on her last visit, she glimpsed a flicker of humor in his eyes. She felt her heart begin a slow, heavy beat of excitement. She wanted to encourage that spark of humor.

"Does your boss know you're here?" he asked.

"Of course." That wasn't strictly true. She'd left a list of the places she was going that day, but Wiley probably wouldn't bother to read it. However, she wasn't responsible for his negligence.

"And he doesn't mind that you're wasting your time?"

She shrugged. "It's my time to waste."

"Honey, it's really the government's time."

"Visiting the ranchers and offering my assistance is part of my job," she answered in a careless tone. "I'm only doing my job."

Luke munched another cookie while he considered. "Since you're determined to help me out even though I don't need your help, and you keep showing up here, why don't you put your money where your mouth is and work with me today?"

His tone told her he thought she couldn't do it— just as he thought she couldn't catch and saddle her own horse when she'd been here before.

She smiled. "I'd love to. After all, what are neighbors for?"

"I've often wondered." He turned away. "Come on. If you're here to help, let's get to work." He glanced back. "And bring the cookies."

With a laugh, Shannon locked the truck after she grabbed her gloves, her lunch and the two-liter bottle of water she'd brought. She could see that his truck was already loaded with tools, cedar posts, staples and wire. Afraid that he might change his mind and decide to leave without her in spite of what he had said, she dashed after him.

When she arrived at the truck in a rush, he glanced up. "Did you think I'd leave without you?"

Color flared into her cheeks, but her eyes sparkled at him as she opened the truck door. "Considering how reluctant you are to take me along, yes. Just remember, you invited me."

"I remember."

"Don't try to back out of it."

"Let's hope you figure out pretty quick that I'm a man of my word, or our future dealings won't be worth much."

Future dealings? That was a big jump from the way he'd shown her the door the last time she'd called. Shannon gave him a swift glance and wondered if he realized what he'd said.

She climbed into the front seat beside him and they started off. The road he took was overgrown with weeds, evidence of its disuse. At least the weeds looked healthy, though, which gave her a spark of hope for this place. A few minutes later, she saw that he'd turned his horses out into one of his few vibrant meadows. They grazed lazily in the late morning sun.

Shannon turned on the bench seat and leaned against the door as she asked, "You plan to hire some hands to help you out around here, don't you?"

The iron set of his jaw told her he didn't like personal questions, but he answered her. "Not yet. I'm doing okay on my own."

"You could do better with help. I know some guys who'd be glad of a job, especially now, while school's out, and—"

"I prefer to work alone."

"I realize that," she said, warming to her subject. "But once you get your operation up and running, I'm sure you're aware as an already experienced rancher that you'll need—"

"If I work alone, I don't have to clean up anybody's mistakes except my own," he interrupted.

Shannon studied his grim profile. She had gone too far. She let her enthusiasm for her job and for this ranch overcome her good sense. It would do no good to antagonize this man. Quickly, she changed her tactics. "I can't believe you admit that you make mistakes," she said in a lighter tone.

"They're rare."

His forbidding expression hadn't changed, but again she heard that spark of humor.

For some reason, her mind insisted on equating those flashes of a better nature with the few signs of verdant growth she saw on the ranch. The two of them were linked, and she felt that encouraging growth in one would help the other.

She knew she should have her head examined for

pursuing this, but she couldn't resist the puzzle he presented. "Let me know if you change your mind about wanting help," she said.

"You'll be the first."

She gave him a look. Too bad he didn't mean that.

Within a few minutes, they had reached the fence between his place and Violet Beardsley's, a mile or so north of the tiny cabin where he'd carried her to recover from her faint.

Luke stopped the truck, and they swung out of the cab and moved to the back. Luke released the tailgate, and Shannon, standing shoulder to shoulder with him, began pulling out equipment in swift, practiced moves.

He paused to watch her set the posthole digger on the ground and grip the handles to test its weight. She glanced up and grinned at the frown on his face. "Don't worry, I know what I'm doing."

Luke took the tool from her. "I'll handle digging postholes," he said, his low voice gruff.

She lifted her chin. "Afraid of a little competition?"

He set the posthole digger on the ground and leaned his forearms on the handles. His eyes were narrow as he answered her. "You keep telling me that you know what you're doing, but I can't believe that someone with your—" his gaze raked over her from the challenge in her eyes to the neat braid that held back her hair, over her flower-patterned shirt and snug jeans to her scarred boots "—other attributes is as competent as you say you are."

That brought a flash of hurt, but Shannon kept her

expression carefully neutral as she said, "That's your problem, then, isn't it? Why don't we get to work?"

He looked as if he wanted to say more, but she turned and grabbed a cedar post. She set it on the end, then arranged several more within easy reach. She would show him, she thought furiously. Pompous, know-it-all, stubborn man. His mind and his attitudes seemed to be mired firmly in the nineteenth century. If she had any sense or pride, she would walk to her truck, drive away and never blight his life again.

But she could be stubborn, too, and she didn't quit when things got rough.

Luke began walking along the fence line, kicking at posts that were rotted from frequent dousing or knocked sideways by floods.

"I realize you don't want my advice on this," she said. "But the flooding along this creek won't solve itself. This wasn't nature-made, and it won't be solved by nature. Other ranchers and environmental groups have tried."

He cut some wire and bent it back from a post. "Well, I'm solving fencing problems today so I can release my horses over here, and if you're here to help, that's what you'll do."

She gritted her teeth. "Whatever you say, boss."

He nodded and set to work. It didn't take her long to catch on to the way he worked, quick and methodical. She made a point of anticipating his needs, handing him staples, hammer, wire cutters before he asked for them. By noon, she was weary and desperately thirsty, but she would never admit it. When they had placed the last staple on the last strand of wire, Luke turned and gave her a look of grudging admiration as he pulled off his gloves.

"You're right," he said abruptly. "You do know what you're doing. Are you ready to eat lunch now?"

"I could eat a whole steer. Raw."

He laughed. "If I had one, I'd feed it to you."

Shannon blinked at his sudden about-face but resisted the urge to remind him she'd told him so. They gathered up their tools and tossed them into the back of the truck. Luke picked up a cooler and brought it to the tailgate while Shannon retrieved her lunch from the cab.

They sat side by side on the tailgate and tucked into their food. Shannon set the bag of cookies between them. As she ate, she swung her feet gently and gazed at Randall Peak and the other, shorter mountains to the south. A breeze swept down from them, stirring the cottonwoods nearby and sending the triangular leaves into a shimmering dance. "I can't imagine living anyplace where I couldn't see mountains," she said, lifting the front of her shirt away from her throat and fanning herself. She took a sip of water and glanced at him. "I know that there are mountains all over Arizona. Which ones were near your home there?"

His gaze lifted to Randall Peak, and he was silent for so long she thought he was going to ignore her. Finally, he said, "The Catalinas. Santa Catalinas. I could see them from my front door." His voice dropped. Shannon went very still as she heard the intense longing in his tone. She looked at him, but he glanced away. After a minute, he cleared his throat.

"That's not unusual, though. You can see them from just about anywhere in Tucson."

"You miss them. Miss your ranch there."

"Yeah."

She couldn't miss the no-trespassing signs in his face and voice, but she also couldn't ignore the faint hint of yearning there. "Why did you sell it, then?"

"Believe me, it wasn't *my* idea. My dad died and...it was sold."

She put down her water bottle and laid her hand over his. "I'm sorry. How long ago was it?"

"Two years."

She wondered fleetingly if it had taken that long to sell the ranch. She knew he'd finalized the purchase of the Crescent very quickly. She suspected the deal had been pushed through by Gus Blackhawk, who feared some member of her family might buy the place.

Luke must have wanted a quick purchase, too, so that he could be alone—maybe even hide out.

She squeezed his hand in compassion. "I lost my father, too, so I know how it feels."

Luke gazed at her small, competent hand resting atop his. She had never been ashamed of the condition of her hands. After all, they were toughened by honest work. Still, for once she wished they were soft and dainty, with long nails polished a bright coral.

Beneath her palm, she could feel his warmth. His gaze met hers.

"Do you?" he asked. Unexpectedly, his hand turned and gripped hers.

She jumped, and her breath caught in her throat.

"Do you know what it's like to lose your father

and find out you're going to lose your ranch all in the same week?''

"Well, no," she said. "I..."

"I don't recommend it," he said, leaning forward. "It can turn a reasonable man into one hell of a bastard."

Flustered, she tried to pull away. "Oh, I don't know about that, I—"

"You want to know how much of a bastard I am, Shannon?" His voice was low and rough.

Fear, excitement and anticipation spiraled through her. It was the first time he'd called her by her first name, but it wasn't spoken in a tone she'd ever wanted to hear. Her mouth went dry, and her heart began a swift, light patter in her throat. Her eyes were fixed on his, and what she saw there frightened her even as it drew her.

Torment. Desire. Rage. She saw all those swirl in his eyes as they drew closer to her own. He tilted his head, and his lips spoke again, only a fraction of an inch from hers.

"I'm enough of a bastard to want to kiss you now. Here. I want to kiss you hard enough to make you furious with me. To want to fight with me. To want to kiss me back. To ruin your opinion of me forever." He laughed that harsh, rusty laugh of his. "Not that I think you've got such a high opinion of me."

Her mouth fell open while heat blossomed in her. No one had ever spoken to her with such raw hunger, heat and need. She had never thought of herself as especially brave, and faced with such intensity, she wanted to run and hide, but this man was hurt, though he would never admit it. His need overcame her fear.

"And you think those are good enough reasons *not* to kiss me?" she asked.

This time, she had been the one to stun him, but she saw it only briefly as he closed the tiny gap between their mouths and did as he had threatened. Their mouths were joined, fused. There was a low, hoarse sound from his throat, or maybe it was hers.

Shannon lifted her hands to grip his shoulders, digging into the rock hard muscles. Her fingers found their way to the back of his neck, eased over the tense muscles there, then plowed into his thick, dark hair. She knocked his cowboy hat over his eye. Impatiently, his hand came up to sweep it off and away. Dizzy, she had no idea where it landed. Then his hands were back, running over her, sweeping the length of her braid.

His lips devoured hers, robbing her of breath and, she knew, of her sanity, because when he turned and urged her onto the bed of the truck, she went willingly. Luke lifted his boot heel onto the tailgate and pushed them both onto the truck bed. With his arms wrapped around her, he eased her onto her back.

The heat from the black truck liner radiated across her shoulders and down her spine, but she barely noticed because she was so involved in matching Luke's passion with her own. She had never known anything like this. Never been kissed with such urgency.

She felt the roughness of his whiskers against her cheek, the firmness of his mouth and teeth bruising her lips. His scent was a combination of spice and sweat and heat. His taste matched it in every point, as if he was pouring the essence of himself into every touch of his mouth on hers.

His lips left hers and raced across her jaw, then down her throat. His hands moved over her, learning the slope of her shoulder, the strength of her arm, the dip of her waist. His fingers grabbed the fabric of her shirt where it disappeared into the waistband of her jeans and began to tug it upward.

That was when sanity returned in a rush. Shannon gulped, tore her lips away from his and placed a hand against his chest.

"Luke," she gasped. "Stop."

He started to chase her lips with his, but she turned her head away, avoiding him. "Luke," she said again, more urgently. "Stop. This has to stop now."

At last, he grew still, and she chanced a look at him. His eyes were dark yet full of fire, his breath coming in short, shallow bursts. She saw a battle going on and for a moment thought he was going to ignore her demand, but he shook his head as if to clear it and squeezed his eyes shut.

When he opened them, he had conquered his desire. Shannon had never seen anyone exercise such willpower. He grasped her shoulders and sat her up, then he slipped off the end of the truck and moved to the fender. Placing his hands on the side of the truck, he dropped his head.

He took a few deep breaths before he looked up. When he did, his eyes were hard and full of self-condemnation as he said, "I told you I was a bastard. Did I hurt you?"

"No."

"Frighten you?"

Shannon pressed her swollen lips together. She scooted to the end of the tailgate and curled her hands over the edge, gripping until her knuckles were white. She dropped her head forward as she struggled to conquer the flurry of emotions that battered her. When she felt steady enough to answer him, she gave her head one quick shake. "No, but things were moving too fast." Her hands lifted in a helpless gesture. "Too strong." Shakily, she stood and began tucking her shirt into her jeans.

He leaned forward and placed his forearms on the side of the truck, letting his hands dangle inside. "Listen, Shannon, I'm not the kind of man, who..." His voice trailed off as his gaze landed on the disturbed dust in the truck bed, then on the places where it had transferred to her shirt. Awkwardly, he reached out and brushed her shoulder as he gave a harsh laugh. "Never mind, I guess I am that kind of man."

A charged silence stretched between them. Shannon didn't know what to say. She'd never before been kissed with such need. She felt as if she'd walked down a long, dark corridor and run smack into a wall. The air was knocked out of her, and her ears were ringing. She couldn't imagine how she had let this happen. She was always so careful to avoid even the appearance of impropriety. In her job, she had to. This had changed everything, altering not only any dealings she might have had with Luke, but her perception of herself.

Maybe she wasn't as smart as she thought she was.

Shaken, Shannon turned and began gathering the remains of her lunch, placing everything into her small cooler. "If we're...finished here, I need to go...back to the office." When she could bring herself to face him, she looked up. ''It seems I've done all I can here.''

''No.'' His caramel-colored eyes met hers. ''No, you haven't. Stay. I'll take you around, and you can show me all that's wrong with this ranch. Tell me how to fix it.''

CHAPTER FOUR

HER eyes widened. This was what she'd wanted all along, but she had to question his motives. "Are you agreeing to this because you feel guilty about..." Her hand fluttered toward the truck bed.

"Yeah." He shrugged. "Not a very noble reason, but there it is."

At least he was honest. That was a good quality, but she suspected it kept him from sparing himself any harshness. If he could be honest, so could she.

"All right. I have to tell you, though, that what happened here can't happen again." Her chin came up. "We have to maintain a professional relationship if we're to work together, and—" this was where things got sticky "—and I must ask you never to tell anyone about..."

"Shannon, I may be a bastard, but I don't kiss and tell."

She felt a blush climbing her cheeks, but she fought it. "All right, then, Luke. I'd be glad to go with you, show you what needs to be done, although we probably can't cover the whole ranch today."

With a businesslike nod, he straightened, tossed the last of his lunch into his cooler and closed the back of the truck while she climbed into the front seat. Their return journey was a silent one. When they reached the corral, Luke caught their horses while she went to get their tack. Once Dusty and Jezebel were saddled, they started off in silence, but after a few minutes, Shannon began to tell him how things could change with years of replanting, careful grazing, work and commitment.

As they rode and talked, Shannon found her mind wandering from her passionate plea for the land. She recalled the passion they had shared in his truck, kisses that, two hours later, were still sending shivers through her. She studied Luke's profile as he gazed at the stream she was describing and wondered how he could be so unaffected.

As if in response to her thought, he turned suddenly to meet her eyes. A flash of awareness told her he wasn't as unaffected as she'd thought. She glanced away, but it took her several stumbling starts to return to the subject of stream runoff.

When they returned to the ranch, it was nearly dark. They took their horses into the corral to unsaddle them. While Luke put away the saddles and bridles, she grabbed a brush and began giving Jezebel a quick but thorough grooming. Luke came to the corral with a bucket of feed in his hand and stopped short.

"What are you doing?"

Shannon straightened and blinked at his gruff tone. "Grooming Jezebel. She's worked hard this afternoon. My dad always said if I take care of my horse, she'll take care of me."

"She's not your horse."

Repressing a sigh of frustration, Shannon said, "She still did everything I asked of her today, so she deserves some pampering." When he didn't respond, she tossed her braid over her shoulder and went back to work. "Don't you usually brush your horse down after you ride for several hours?"

"If I have time."

"Then what's the matter?"

"I was surprised, that's all. I usually do things on my own. I'm not used to people pitching in."

As if she hadn't figured that out already, Shannon thought, and felt a sad wrench in her heart. Another little bit of the puzzle dropped into place. He didn't ask for help because he didn't expect it. He was the most *alone* man she had ever met.

By the time they had finished with the horses, dark had fallen, cloaking the ranch buildings in blue and lavender shadows. Luke clicked on a tall light at the corner of the barn as they walked across the yard. It didn't do much to illuminate the way to the main ranch house, a big rock structure with wraparound porches, or to the two smaller dwellings behind it.

Shannon was pleasantly tired and ravenously hungry. She was planning to stop by her mother's house on the way home and beg some dinner. She knew she would be welcomed, fussed over, fed.

She cast a sidelong glance at Luke, who strolled silently beside her, and felt a pang of regret that there was no one to do that for him. Not that he appeared to want anyone to fuss over him. Still, it must be hard to work alone all day and then go into an empty house every night.

Shannon gave herself a mental shake. Maybe it didn't bother him. Not everyone was as gregarious and anxious for enjoyable company as she was. Perhaps he preferred his own company.

"Would you like to come in?" Luke asked. Shannon started, feeling as if he'd read her mind—and proven her wrong. "I have a few more questions I'd like to ask you. I'll get us something to drink."

"I'd like that," Shannon said, surprised to find herself anticipating a look inside his home. When she started automatically for the porch steps to the main house, he laid a hand on her arm.

"Not there. I live around back. This place is too big for me," he added by way of explanation.

"Oh. I see." She gave the house a faintly regretful look. She had heard so much about the legendary Crescent house, and she would love to take a peek inside.

Luke led the way to one of the small houses behind the main one and flipped on the living room light as they entered. He hung his hat on a rack by the door, and Shannon did the same, then smoothed her hair as she made a quick scan of the place.

It told her very little about him. The room held a sofa, softly padded, long enough for a man to stretch out for a nap—not that she thought he ever napped—and upholstered in brown cordovan leather. It faced a wood-burning stove, as did the matching recliner. There was no television, only a small clock radio to bring the outside world into the room. There were few personal articles around, except for a picture of a man and woman on the mantelpiece. Shannon assumed that it was Luke's father and mother. She wanted to stop and examine it, ask more about them, but he didn't pause.

Luke pointed her to the bathroom in case she wanted to freshen up. Shannon was grateful for the offer and found the room as stark, clean and utilitarian as the rest of the house. She knew that if she snooped and opened the medicine cabinet, she would see the bare essentials in personal grooming aids, a razor, shaving cream, toothbrush and toothpaste. She doubted that she would find cologne, but surely a bottle of after-shave to account for that uniquely spicy scent of his that enthralled her so much.

When she joined Luke in the kitchen, he was standing by the counter, legs crossed at the ankles, arms crossed over his chest. One hand held a long-necked bottle of beer. He looked up when she entered, his gaze sweeping over her, then lingering on her face.

Shannon paused, one hand on the doorjamb. Her midnight blue eyes studied him. In a flash, she again recalled when he had kissed her earlier that day. They'd managed to avoid any reference to it all afternoon, but the sudden, intense light in his eyes made her wonder if he would bring it up now. But his eyelids dropped, hiding his eyes and his thoughts, leaving Shannon feeling vaguely disappointed.

"Would you like a beer?" he asked, indicating the bottle he held.

"No, thanks. I'm not really much of a drinker. Ice water would be fine with me."

With a nod, he got it for her, then invited her to sit at the oak table in the corner. He wandered over to join her and began asking more questions.

"I won't kid you, Luke," she said after she had answered everything. "This won't be easy, and it will take a huge infusion of cash. If your ranch becomes part of our project, though, there are grants available that could help."

"Grants? Government grants?" he asked warily.

"That's right."

His eyebrows snapped together. "No. Government money means government strings I don't want."

"You've got government strings now," she pointed out. "You've got to follow government rules and regulations, meet federal standards."

"That's part of industry regulations. I expect that. It just makes good business sense to follow those. I won't have bureaucrats on my land, though."

Shannon's heart sank. "Luke, technically, *I'm* a bureaucrat."

"Yeah, well, you're not like the others I've met, with a shiny bald head and an insufferable ego."

"Look," she persisted. "Having you, a rancher, a true cattleman, want the place intact, and not subdivided into mini ranchettes was like having it rescued from the path of a speeding train."

Luke's light brown eyes studied her. "I'm not some hero riding up on a white horse. I didn't buy it for any noble reasons."

"I know that, but if you become part of our project, there will be people to help you get it into shape. It's a unique opportunity for...for the future, for you to get to know people here, settle into the community."

"I thought I'd made it clear that I can manage on my own."

Shannon sat back, dropped her hands into her lap and let her shoulders droop. She felt as if she was trying to push a rock uphill. "Yes," she answered wearily. "You did make that clear, I was just hoping you would change your mind. You know, what occurs here on the Crescent affects the ranches and communities nearby. It's a very involved ecosystem.''

His eyes shifted from hers, but then his gaze steadied. His voice was deep and measured as he said, ''I'll do what I can on my own.''

She threw her hands into the air. ''Won't you change your mind?''

''Probably not in this lifetime.''

The harsh words sank the last of her hope. It would do no good to argue. That would only irritate him. Accepting it sadly, Shannon stood and carried her glass to the sink. ''Then I'm wasting my time here. I'd better go.'' She turned with a brittle smile. Disappointment was bitter on her tongue as she said, ''Thanks for letting me look over the Crescent. I've been fascinated by it for years. I guess I won't be seeing you again—at least, not in my official capacity.'' Her eyes darted around the room, avoiding his. ''If you should need something, though, please call my office. Goodbye.'' Her boot heels pummeled the wooden floor as she started from the room.

''Shannon, wait.'' Luke surged out of his chair and laid his hand on her arm.

Startled by the gesture and by the heat of his hand, Shannon stumbled to a halt. Unbidden, memories of the heat of both his hands as they had cupped her skin flashed through her. She drew in a breath that felt as rough as the business end of a saw blade. She was stunned to see his gaze flickering over her face as if he was trying to think of what to say, give a reason for having stopped her.

''I saw you looking at the main house as we walked by. Would you like to see inside?''

She was so surprised by the offer, she could only stare. "The...the house?"

He nodded once, quickly, as if he wanted her to agree immediately, before he changed his mind.

Actually, it was the last thing she wanted to do. She wanted to hurry away from this place, to get her mental bearings, to put this disturbing man and the death of her hopes behind her, but it might be her only opportunity to see the house. She had heard so much about it over the years but had never been inside. She found herself agreeing in a faint voice. "Sure, Luke. I'd like that."

"I'll get the key."

Was that relief she saw in his eyes? Shannon wondered as he turned away. She thought he would be anxious to be rid of her, of her interference and opinions. Confused, she trailed after him as he removed the key from a desk in the corner of the living room, then held the door for her.

They were silent as they crossed the yard to the big house, and Shannon put aside her questions as Luke unlocked the door, which boasted a Tiffany-style glass panel she suspected was genuine. Luke turned on the lights and stood back for her to enter.

Stepping inside the famous Crescent Ranch house, Shannon felt as if she'd slipped back forty years in time.

It was an old-fashioned ranch house with the bird's-eye maple floors she'd heard about. They echoed beneath her feet as she moved. At the end of the entryway, there was a sturdy wooden staircase with a carved banister that led to the second floor and big, square windows deep set in the rock walls.

There were no rugs or furnishings, but she could imagine how it must have looked at one time, the big rooms graced by the wood and leather furniture unique to the west, braided rugs on the floor, practical fabric curtains at the windows. The stories she'd heard about crystal chandeliers weren't true. The fixtures were plain but fit the rooms perfectly.

She turned in a slow circle, seeing the place as it must have once been. A tingle ran up her spine. She could almost hear it ringing with the sound of children's voices as they played or fussed with each other.

"Come on, you guys, let's go play. I'm not It!"

"Mama, he hid my doll. Make him give it back."

The imaginary sounds died as suddenly as they had sprung up in her mind, leaving only the sigh of the wind as it swept through the open door. Shannon shivered at her fanciful notion and glanced at Luke to see if he'd noticed her reaction.

Relieved, she saw that he was moving around the room, checking to make sure the windows were securely locked. He paused before a big rock fireplace at one end of the room and gazed into the blackened, empty grate.

Shannon imagined a dying fire there, a late-at-night, it's-time-for-bed fire. Her mind saw him turning, holding out his hand and saying, "The kids are asleep, at last. I thought those little outlaws would never drop off. Are you ready for bed?" There was a warm, sexy smile in his eyes and on his lips. A smile that told her the journey to bed wouldn't include sleep for a while. A smile meant only for her.

A gasp escaped her throat, and Luke turned suddenly to study her. "Something wrong?"

"No." She cleared her throat, wishing she could clear her head as easily. She was famous for being practical and down-to-earth and had never been subject to such fanciful notions before. She could only accredit it to being tired and hungry. "No. I'm fine," she said, but her smile was shaky.

She strolled into the dining room, which was furnished with two huge sideboards that looked as if they could have come from an English hunting lodge, and a beautiful walnut table, long enough to seat fourteen comfortably. The matching chairs were upended on the top.

The kitchen held an old-fashioned gas range with eight burners and a separate grill. Glass-fronted cabinets straight out of the 1940s stood empty. The room had a big double sink but no modern conveniences. She was surprised, but oddly pleased to see that the room had never been updated.

It was the same story upstairs, with claw-footed tubs and pedestal-style sinks in the bathrooms. The bedrooms were furnished. When she commented on it, Luke shrugged.

"Look at this stuff," he said, pointing to a huge mahogany bed and dresser that crowded the master bedroom. "Who could move it? It was left here because no one wanted to break their backs getting it down those stairs." He shook his head. "I suspect the house was built around it."

Shannon laughed and glanced around again. In one corner, she saw a baby cradle. It was carved and curlicued and had a fat little rabbit painted on the end.

Looking at it, Shannon felt the same strange tremor she'd experienced a few minutes before. Her mind pictured Luke holding it, turning to her, grinning invitingly and saying, "Don't you think it's about time to fill this thing up again? Seems like a crime to have it just sitting here, gathering dust."

"No," Luke said, stepping into her line of vision as he moved around the room. "I'm not touching any of this stuff yet. It's been sitting here for years. It can sit a little longer."

Unnerved, Shannon wondered if she was suffering from some kind of hallucination. This house was having a strange effect on her. She put a hand to her temple.

"Yes, yes, of course," she said vaguely. She turned suddenly and headed downstairs. "Thanks for...for the tour, Luke. It's time for me to go." Even as she said the words, she wished she didn't have to. She put that crazy longing down to a moment of weakness brought on by exhaustion and hunger.

If Luke noticed her sudden haste, he didn't comment. He followed her to the truck. When she was inside, he closed the door, then leaned his hands on it.

Shannon paused as she reached for the ignition. She wanted to give this one more try. "Luke," she said, turning so she could see him in the glow of the yard light. "The local cattlemen's group is having their regular meeting next week." She told him where and when. "I always go because it keeps me informed about what's happening in the community. If you'd like to come, you'd be welcome."

Luke stared at her for several seconds. "I'll keep it in mind," he responded.

She knew he wouldn't. She also knew that, except for chance meetings in town, she probably wouldn't see him again. After she drove out tonight, she wouldn't return unless she was invited. There would be no reason to. Her heart sank at the thought, but she put on a professional smile. "Well, good night, then." Her hand trembled, and her muscles felt watery as she started the truck and pulled out.

She glanced in the rearview mirror and saw him standing where she'd left him. Hands resting on his lean waist, his head bent as if he was studying the ground before him, he was a solitary figure. She turned into the long drive leading to the highway, blocking out the lonely sight.

As he watched the taillights of Shannon's truck disappear down the drive, Luke felt something stir inside him. He'd been alone for so long, known only his own company for so many weeks before and after moving to Colorado, that at first he didn't recognize the feelings as regret and loneliness.

With a sound of disgust, he spun on his heel and stalked toward the corral. He couldn't have her around. Hadn't he learned his lesson already? Hadn't he learned that the more he gave, the more he lost? And that applied to everything—home, property, emotions. Everything he had, he would keep for himself. He wasn't going to have interference from even the most well-meaning government agency. He was certainly going to obey the law, but he wouldn't have anyone on his place telling him what he could and couldn't do. If that made him a selfish bastard, then so be it. He'd learned the hard way that it was the only way he could survive.

Luke checked the corral gate, then the barn, though he wasn't sure why he bothered. It was empty and would stay that way until he could get the roof repaired. That was a job he could do himself, and he really didn't care if it took a few weeks. He had time. In fact, time and this ranch were about all he did have.

Turning, he headed to the house, struck as always by the incongruity of the tiny bungalow huddled behind the great hulk of the main house. It was a comfortable place for a solitary man, which was what he intended to remain. He wasn't going to entertain thoughts of having a woman there, especially not one like Shannon Kelleher, no matter how beautiful or smart or determined she might be. And he wasn't going to torture himself with memories of having her there, looking around the rooms, sitting at his table drinking ice water.

Luke scraped his feet on the rough sisal doormat before going inside. Living alone had quickly taught him that if he didn't want to sweep dirt and barn muck out of the house, he'd better not bring it in.

He reached automatically to remove his hat, then realized he wasn't wearing one. His hand fell away slowly as he glanced at the hat rack. His hat was there, and so was Shannon's.

There was no way he could have stopped the spark of hope that shot through him at the thought of her coming back to retrieve it, but Luke shoved it aside ruthlessly.

He plucked Shannon's hat from the rack and turned

it in his hands. It was felt, a light tan and with a smaller crown and brim. A woman's hat, not an expensive one like his best one, a handmade beaver, but still a good hat with a brim wide enough to keep the sun off of that creamy skin of hers. He pictured her in it, riding Jezebel as she had today, one hand going up to hold it as they had arrived at the top of Randall Peak and the wind had whipped around them.

She had lifted herself in the stirrups, pointing down the side of the slope. The action had stretched her shirt over her tiny waist and her full breasts. Heat had rushed through him, jolting him into realizing he was having feelings he never expected to experience for a range manager. She hadn't noticed the lecherous way he'd watched her or much of anything else. She'd been too involved in talking about runoff, soil conservation, the tin-roof effect. Hell, who'd have thought listening to her talk about such subjects would have been such a turn-on?

Luke lifted the hat to his face, upended it and sniffed the inside, feeling foolish even as he did it. He didn't care, though, as soon as her scent drew him in.

That was it, he thought, closing his eyes briefly. That was the scent he'd smelled and tasted on her. It was a citrusy, no-nonsense but all-woman aroma that had teased him since he'd climbed down from his barn roof and stood before her. This was what he'd tasted when he'd kissed her today—which should be written in the record books as one of the world's most stupid mistakes.

With a disgusted sound aimed at himself, Luke hung her hat beside his and went into the kitchen. He

opened the refrigerator and began pulling out sandwich makings, which was all he seemed to eat lately.
He'd lost pounds, his jeans were loose in the waist,
and he couldn't have cared less. He'd had a cook and
housekeeper in Arizona, but Dolores had retired when
the ranch was sold, and he hadn't bothered hiring anyone since he'd moved. A bachelor determined to live
and work alone could do for himself.

He slathered mustard on bread and tossed a couple
of slices of ham on top. Jamming the stack together,
he chewed and swallowed methodically, washing it
down with milk.

Sandwich in one hand, glass in the other, he wandered to the doorway and looked across the room at
the hat rack.

He was avoiding the issue, he knew. He'd have to
deal with it head-on and resolve it. Either he took the
hat back to her or Shannon would return for it. He
didn't want either one to happen, but he wasn't the
type to wait for something to happen if he could affect
the outcome. It was a trait he'd been born with and
one that had been reinforced by the events of the past
two years.

Shannon would get her hat back, and soon, then he
would make sure he was left alone to work and to
live his life.

Luke finished his sandwich and turned to make another.

No matter how lonely that life might be.

Shannon set a chocolate cake she had baked on a table
already groaning with bowls, plates and platters of
food, then turned to survey the big meeting room of

the community center. Smiling, she greeted friends and neighbors, including some newcomers. There were always a few at the annual summer get-together, and Shannon usually took the opportunity to make new contacts. The more ranchers she could get involved in her project, the better her data and results would be.

A frown crossed her face when she spotted Wiley Frost across the room. He hadn't been happy that Luke Farraday had refused to be part of the project. He'd viewed it as a personal failing of Shannon's, though she didn't see it that way. Luke simply wanted to be left alone, and she'd told Wiley they should respect that. He'd countered that having the Crescent Ranch in the project would be a real feather in their caps. Shannon was no fool. She'd known he meant *his* cap. If Wiley had his way, her cap would be nowhere in sight.

Just as her hat wasn't, she thought ruefully.

She was going to have to go back to get it. She needed it. She wore it almost every day. It was her favorite. Even though Luke had made it clear that he didn't want her on his place, she felt a rush of anticipation at the idea of seeing him again. All she would have to do was go, get her hat, pass the time of day, ask after his health and leave. She didn't have to think about the time they'd spent together or the way he'd kissed her.

She spent too much time doing that already.

With a wry twist to her lips, Shannon lifted her cup and glanced toward the open door.

Luke Farraday stood there, surveying the room, his face calm and unsmiling, his light brown eyes surveying the crowd. She blinked, wondering if her thoughts had conjured him up. Her gaze skimmed over him. He looked wonderful in a navy blue Western shirt with a snap front, black jeans and boots. Was it her imagination, or did he seem to dominate that area of the room? Did it seem that people were turning toward him, falling silent as they regarded this stranger in their midst?

CHAPTER FIVE

LUKE'S gaze moved around the room, then stopped and focused on her as if she'd called his name. But she knew she hadn't said a thing. A tingle of awareness traveled up her spine and down her arms. His eyes took in the turquoise cotton sweater she wore with a matching patterned skirt. It was her favorite outfit, and as she watched Luke surveying it, she was passionately glad she'd worn it tonight.

His eyes traveled to her feet in their strappy black sandals. Uncharacteristically, she'd painted her toe-nails bright coral. She should have felt foolish, but instead she thought it made her seem daring and feminine.

Shakily, she set her punch cup on a nearby table and started toward him. People fell silent as she passed, a phenomenon she'd never experienced in this crowd. Their attention followed her.

When she reached Luke, she held out her hand. "Hello, Luke, I'm so glad you could make it. Come in and meet everyone."

His eyes fixed on her face, one brow lifted slightly, he asked, "Is this some kind of party? I thought you said it was a meeting. I only came so I could return your hat." His head tilted toward the parking lot. "It's in the truck."

"Oh." Vaguely, she glanced at the people nearby, all of whom were silent and listening. Heat flushed

73

her face. She felt like the prize goldfish in the bowl. "Thank you for returning it. I...I guess I forgot to tell you that tonight is the annual summer get-together. Everyone brings food, and..." She pressed her lips together. The truth was, she hadn't expected him to come, so she hadn't thought it necessary to mention it.

"I didn't bring anything." His deep voice rumbled. "I'm not much of a cook."

He stepped back as if he intended to turn and leave, but Shannon moved quickly to take his arm. The iron-hard muscles flexed beneath her fingers. "No one would have expected you to. You're a guest. Come in."

She smiled at him, her dark blue eyes clear with the pleasure and anticipation she felt at seeing him. For a moment, she feared he would refuse, but as he looked at her, she saw something shift in his eyes, a momentary softening that made her tighten her hand on his arm. Hope warmed her. "Please," she said. "Come in."

Just then her mother stepped forward, smiling, and asked Shannon to introduce her. As she did so, Shannon felt a flurry of love and pride. Her mother was beautiful, with her blond hair and soft gray eyes and her warm, welcoming manner.

"Mr. Farraday, how nice to meet you. I'm happy that we're neighbors. Come meet everyone." She placed her hand on his arm and smiled into his face.

He glanced at Shannon, and she wondered if he'd expected to slip in and out of the meeting unnoticed. But not even the hardest heart could resist Mary Jane's warmth and friendliness.

With a nod, he said, "It's nice to meet you, Mrs. Kelleher." He let the two women draw him in. Within minutes, Shannon had pressed a cup of punch into his hand, though his eyes had mocked her. She knew he would have preferred beer, but the group had an agreement that none would be served until after the meeting.

Luke met the people who owned property bordering his and was listening to a discussion of the new grazing fees being considered by the federal government.

Wiley sidled up to introduce himself. "I'm Shannon's boss," he said, showing his teeth. "We talked on the phone a couple of weeks ago."

"I remember," Luke answered, his eyes cool.

Wiley blinked as if he couldn't figure out why Luke wasn't greeting him with a hearty slap on the back. "Well, uh, sounds like Shannon didn't make you an attractive enough offer to get you in on our project. If she didn't offer what you need, we can arrange something."

Embarrassment rushed through Shannon. Was it her imagination, or was he trying to inject some kind of sexual undertone into his offer? She certainly understood that he was putting her down in front of Luke.

Luke didn't even blink. His eyes narrowed as they traveled over Wiley, then fixed on the man's oily smile. "Are you a range management specialist?"

"Well, no," Wiley answered. The truth was, he didn't have half her education or experience. He drew himself up, reminding Shannon of a bantam rooster.

"I'm the boss, though, so anything she does has to be approved by me."

"That's too bad." Luke's tone was matter-of-fact. "If I need help, I prefer to deal with professionals and experts."

Wiley blinked at him as he realized that he'd been the one put in his place. His eyes narrowed, and Shannon felt a frisson of alarm. Luke regarded Wiley calmly. Wiley responded in a brittle voice. "All right, Farraday," he said. "Let us know if you need anything."

As he turned away, Wiley's eyes snapped angrily, but not at Luke. He was mad at Shannon, and she knew she'd pay for it one way or another tomorrow. She could handle that, though. She handled it every day. Besides, it was satisfying to see Wiley at a loss.

"Weasel," Luke commented and dismissed him. He looked at her, a slight smile on his lips. "I assume the uncle who hired him is as weasly as he is."

She hid her grin by biting her bottom lip. "I'm afraid so."

"Any chance somebody'll boot him out and you can take over his job?"

"Not much." She gave him a sidelong glance. "Does your interest mean you'll reconsider?"

"I might," he answered, surprising her, then heaped on frustration by not pursuing it. He glanced around the room. "Let's find a seat. Looks like they're about to get this show on the road."

The meeting was called to order, and people found chairs and began to sit. Shannon was pleased when he touched her elbow to guide her to a seat, then sat next to her.

The meeting was short because everyone wanted to get to the food and dancing. Discussions ranged from federal grazing fees to beef prices. Many people expressed frustration that they couldn't affect these important aspects of their business.

Shannon noticed that Luke listened carefully, his head tilted. She wondered if he was comparing this group to ones he'd attended in Arizona. She knew from talking to her colleagues that there wasn't much difference in the concerns of ranchers to the south of them.

When the meeting was over, the chairs were moved to surround the tables that had been set up, the food was served, and the noise level rose to deafening proportions.

Shannon and Luke took their plates and escaped to a far corner of the room. Laughing, Shannon sat with a whoosh of breath. "It's not always like this," she promised. "Just twice a year, summer and Christmas. Did you belong to a cattlemen's group in Arizona?"

"Yeah." Luke picked up a saltshaker and carefully salted his food. "Though it was shrinking every year. Fewer ranchers because of fewer ranches. They're pretty much being chewed up by developers."

Shannon nodded. He didn't say, "Including mine," but she knew that's what he was thinking. Curiosity compelled her to ask, "Why did you sell, Luke? It seems to bother you so much...."

Her words died at the fierce light in his eyes. "What makes you think it was my idea?" he asked.

Feeling herself skating close to the edge, Shannon considered dropping the question, but she'd spent too much time in the past week thinking and wondering about him. "Because you always talk about it as if it was your ranch."

Luke picked up a knife and spread butter on his bread. "I thought it was, until I found out my father had put it jointly in his name and my stepmother's. He thought she'd do the right thing, stay on the place, let me run it, then turn it over to me in a couple of years." Luke glanced up. "He was wrong. I tried to stop her with legal maneuvers, but the court said she had the right to sell." Luke's cool gaze landed on her. "And I guarantee you that one way or another, Catherine usually gets what she wants. So she sold, split her hefty profits with me, took the money and moved to Phoenix. She did give me enough to buy the place here. The Willow Springs ranch had been in my family for sixty years. She sold it. End of story." The short, staccato sentences were rapped out tonelessly. He expected no pity and he gave none to the stepmother who had betrayed him.

Shannon sat, stunned, as every conversation she'd had with him came clear in the light of this revelation. He felt betrayed by those he'd been closest to so now he wouldn't let anyone get close enough to threaten what he had. She was at a loss to know what to say. A glance at his guarded expression told her he didn't expect her to say anything, or want her to. The subject was closed.

Shannon stood in the pool of light that illuminated the parking lot of the neighborhood hall and stared down the road. She tucked her hands into her skirt pockets as a troubled frown drew a line between her brows. This time she was the one looking at the tail-lights of a truck as it disappeared in the distance. Luke had taken his leave immediately after eating, saying he had chores to attend to. She suspected he had left because he was angry with himself for telling her as much as he had. Shannon thought he had given her a precious gift, because such a private man didn't share things easily.

Shannon turned and started into the hall, her steps slow.

Without a doubt, she knew he didn't want pity. That wasn't what she felt, though. Her heart was heavy with the truth of what had happened to him. She felt sorrow, but also admiration for the way he had picked himself up and started again. It added another intriguing dimension to the picture she was forming of him.

Shannon went over the things she knew about Luke—strong, gruff yet compassionate, a hard worker, someone who preferred to be left alone. She was beginning to sort out which of those character-istics were inborn and which had been thrust upon him. The fact that he'd shown up tonight was proof, at least to her, that he wasn't as determined to be a loner as he liked to think he was. He'd seemed per-fectly at ease and interested in the discussions at to-night's meeting.

She thought that bringing back her hat was just an excuse to... Shannon stopped and turned with a laugh as she looked down the deserted road. He'd left in such a hurry that he'd forgotten to return her hat. It was still in his truck.

Happiness bubbled through her. Now she had an

excuse to go see him. If the opportunity rose, she could talk to him about the conservation project again, but if it didn't she would still get to see him. That was reason enough, as far as she was concerned.

Shannon stepped out of the agency truck the next morning humming a catchy tune. She had awakened in a happy mood, full of hopes for the day. She had dressed in her usual work jeans and boots, but instead of the long-sleeved shirt she normally wore to keep the sun from burning her arms, she'd put on a sleeveless one and slathered on tons of sunscreen. The navy blue and white striped shirt looked fresh and crisp, and because of all the hard work she did, she had great muscle tone in her upper arms. Why not show it off? She had also done her hair differently, pulling a few loose tendrils from the French braid around her face and curling them softly.

Shannon had decided to admit, at least to herself, that she was attracted to Luke Farraday as she had never before been attracted to a man. Besides, he had already seen her at her worst, when she had fainted at his feet. Last night and today might make a better impression.

As she closed the truck door, she glanced around for Luke. His truck was parked beside the house, and Dusty was in the corral, so she thought he must be working somewhere nearby. She strolled toward the barn.

Pausing just inside the door, she waited for her eyes to become accustomed to the dimness. She heard a faint sound, almost like a cat's cry.

She didn't think too much about it until it came

again, louder, and she realized it wasn't a cat. Alarmed, she hurried into the barn, searching for the source, wondering if it could be a hurt animal.

As her eyes adjusted to the dimness, she spied Luke. He was standing by one of the stalls. A couple of hay bales were stacked in front of him, and he appeared to be leaning forward, holding something in his hand.

"Luke, is something wrong? I heard...." Her words died away as his head jerked up. He whirled around, and she saw what he was holding.

It was a baby bottle, and propped up on the hay bales was an infant seat—and an infant.

Shannon's mouth opened and shut a couple of times as she took in the scene. If the sight of him with a baby wasn't enough to surprise her, the complete discomfort in his expression would have done it. The baby bottle appeared as out of place in his big, rough hand as a pink bow would have looked around the neck of a bull elk.

She snapped her mouth shut and swallowed. Her gaze went from his surprised face to the crying baby. Tiny fists beat the air as the baby's body stiffened in outrage. "Something tells me this isn't yours," she said.

He gave her a harassed look. "My nephew."

The baby began to wail louder, and Shannon stepped closer. "I didn't know you had a nephew."

"*I* didn't even know until last night." He gave the baby a worried look and made another attempt at giving him the bottle. The baby turned his head from side to side rapidly, avoiding the nipple. He screwed his little face up and cried lustily.

"What?" Shannon asked, flabbergasted. "What did you say?"

Awkwardly, Luke set the bottle down and began fumbling with the straps that held the baby in the infant seat. "My half sister, Jeanette, was here when I got home last night. She brought the baby with her. His name's Cody. She says he's two months old."

Luke picked the baby up under the arms. Cody dangled from Luke's hands like a load of wet wash from a line. He was dressed in a one-piece pajama outfit, and through the soft knit, Shannon could see that his diaper was bunched and drooping around his tiny hips. Vaguely, she wondered if Luke had ever changed a diaper before he'd put that one on his nephew.

Man and baby looked into each other's eyes. Cody stopped crying and brought his fist to his mouth as he stared into his uncle's agitated face. Seemingly unimpressed with the job Luke was doing, he started crying again, his feet kicking in rage. Whatever his needs were, they weren't being met. Luke gave Shannon a helpless look.

Taking pity on him, she reached for the baby and cradled him in one arm. With the practiced motion of one who'd spent her high-school years baby-sitting and the past few helping with a niece and nephew, she tucked the baby against her chest and picked up the bottle. It was ice-cold.

"Luke, he won't drink this because it's too cold. Didn't you warm it?"

He shifted his feet and jutted out his jaw. "Sure. Even I know that much, but it took so long to get all his stuff together and get out here, I guess it got cold again.''

''Why did you come out here?''

''Thought he might go to sleep after he ate and I could get some work done.'' He lifted anxious eyes to her. ''Don't they usually do that?''

''Usually,'' Shannon admitted. ''But probably not in a barn.''

''Oh.''

Cody started to cry again, his face plunging against her blouse hungrily. With a laugh, she held him away. ''Something tells me your sister's been nursing him. Which is what she'd better do right now. Where is she? In the house?''

''By now, I'd say she's probably halfway to Texas.''

''What?''

Luke began to gather the baby's things. ''It's a long story. Let's go into the house and I'll tell you all about it.''

''I can't wait to hear this.'' Shannon held Cody against her shoulder and hurried from the barn. Luke followed, the baby carrier dangling incongruously from one hand, a diaper bag in the other, his face a mask of masculine distress.

In the house, Shannon worked quickly to open the bottle and pop it into the microwave. While it warmed, she laid the baby on the table. ''He needs a diaper change,'' she said as she unsnapped his suit.

''I just changed him,'' Luke said, an edge of frustration to his voice. ''That's a fresh diaper.''

''And it's about to fall off.''

He shuffled his feet again. ''Well, I'm new at this.''

Shannon hid her smile and resisted the urge to say, "No kidding." "You'll learn," she told him. "It takes practice." When he stared at her, she prompted, "A diaper, Luke."

"Uh, yeah, right. A diaper." Luke unzipped the bag and began rooting around. He pulled one out and slapped it into her hand. "Putting a diaper on him is harder than branding a calf. And he's got no hips. How does he keep his pants up if he's got no hips?"

Shannon's blue eyes sparkled at the mystified expression on his face. "Well, he can't. He depends on us to do that for him. Look." Efficiently, she laid the diaper under Cody, separated the tapes, pulled the front up and the back forward. "The secret is to get it snug enough just under his belly button so that it won't fall off, but not so tight that he's uncomfortable when his tummy's full."

"So you're saying it's a judgment call every time?"

"Only until you've had enough practice to tell by feel." She grinned, demonstrating by tucking her forefinger into the front of Cody's diaper to test its snugness.

He looked at her in horror. "I'm not sticking my finger in any diaper!"

"This from a man who cleans up after horses all day," she muttered. She stuffed Cody's small legs into his suit and snapped it up. He was the same age as Christina, but he was longer and more active, so she had to struggle a bit to get him dressed. When she was finished, she handed him to Luke then turned to take the bottle from the microwave, stir it carefully and replace the lid. She tested the temperature on her wrist and found it acceptable.

Luke shook his head. "You'll have to show me again. You did that diaper change fast."

"Let's feed him first." She placed the nipple in the hungry baby's mouth and glanced around. "You don't have a rocking chair, do you?"

"Will he start crying again if you don't rock him while you feed him?" Luke asked, eyeing the baby as if he was a time bomb set to explode.

"I really don't know."

Luke took off his hat, which he'd worn throughout the diaper changing, and ran his hand through his hair. "Great. That's just great. I...wait. There's one upstairs in the main house. I'll go get it." He clapped his hat onto his head and dashed for the door as if he was on his way to save the universe from destruction.

Laughing softly, Shannon carried Cody into the living room and sat in Luke's big leather recliner to wait for him. While the baby drank, she had a moment to study him. He was a beautiful boy with long feathery lashes over his deep blue eyes and a soft frizz of gingery-red hair.

"Looks like you were quite a surprise to your uncle Luke, little one," she whispered. She had been taken aback by seeing Luke with a baby and touched by his earnest attempts to take care of him. She loved seeing this new side to Luke. His cool, distant attitude had been blasted away, and she wasn't sorry to see it go.

By the time Luke returned, Cody had drunk nearly two ounces of formula, testifying to how hungry he'd been. Luke carried the rocking chair in, wiped off the dust with a kitchen towel, then moved it to a corner of the room, away from drafts.

Carefully, Shannon carried Cody to the chair and settled in to finish feeding him. After they were comfortable, Luke collapsed into his recliner and took a gasping breath as if he'd been hit by a tidal wave and washed onto a rocky beach. As Shannon watched in amusement, he pulled out a handkerchief and wiped his forehead.

"So, how did you fall heir to little Cody here?" she asked when it looked as if Luke had calmed down.

Luke laughed mirthlessly and shook his head. "It was one of the biggest surprises of my life. I got home last night to see my sister's car parked in front of the main house. She was sitting on the porch waiting for me. You could have knocked me over with a feather when I saw that she was carrying that little bundle."

"You hadn't seen her in a while, I guess?" Shannon spread a clean cloth diaper on her shoulder and lifted Cody to rock him gently as she burped him.

"Not in more than a year. My stepmother, Catherine, took Jeanette along to Phoenix, where she used the money from the sale of the ranch to buy herself a condo and the ritzy life-style she'd always wanted."

"Did Jeanette like that life-style?"

"She says she did at first, but when she graduated from high school and wanted to be on her own, Catherine refused to let her go or give her much of the money."

Shannon sat up straight. "High school? Just how old is this sister of yours?"

"She turned nineteen last month."

"Good grief," Shannon said faintly. A child having a child, she thought, then said, "Sorry I interrupted. Go on."

"She had her own car and a little money, so she left and started following the rodeo circuit."

"Does she compete?"

"Nah, just follows the circuit, dangles after the cowboys." Luke made a disgusted sound. "Dad would have had a fit if he'd known about it."

Ditto for Luke, Shannon thought, studying the fierce expression on his face. He didn't look at all happy with his sister's choice of being what the rodeo cowboys called a buckle bunny.

"Anyway, she met a bronc rider named Steve, fell in love with him, or so she says, and ended up with little Cody there—though the two of them didn't bother to get married."

"Where was your stepmother while all this was going on?"

"Chasing them around the country trying to convince Jeanette to come home—until Jeanette got pregnant, that is. Then Catherine didn't want anything to do with her."

"You're kidding," Shannon gasped. "Why ever not?"

Luke's lips thinned. "I guarantee you that, as much as Catherine wants to get her own way, she doesn't like the idea of being a grandmother. She probably thought that if she ignored it, it would go away."

Shannon looked at the baby nestled against her shoulder. His stillness told her he had fallen asleep. She left him where he was, enjoying the feel of snug-

gling his tiny body. She couldn't imagine his grandmother turning her back on him, but she didn't doubt
Luke's word.

"Before Cody was born, Steve got a place for them
in Albuquerque. He stuck with the circuit and was
gone most of the time, but he sent his winnings to
Jeanette. Yesterday, Jeanette got a call that he'd been
injured at a rodeo in Texas. It's pretty bad. He's in
the hospital there. She had to go to him, but there was
no one to take care of Cody."

Shannon looked up, her eyes shining with amusement. "So Uncle Luke got the job."

"Looks like." His baffled expression said he still
didn't understand quite how that had happened. "Uncle Luke," he whispered, stunned.

"She knew she could trust you."

"Yeah, well, maybe her trust was misplaced," he
answered, eyeing the sleeping baby dubiously. "I
mean, if I can't even change a diaper right, this isn't
going to work out very well."

"You'll learn, and probably very quickly."

"I'd better. She may be gone for a couple of
weeks."

Shannon stood. "I think he's settled down to sleep.
Does he have a bed?"

Luke showed her to the tiny second bedroom where
a small travel crib was set up beside the bed. She laid
Cody down and patted his back for a few minutes,
then covered him and left the room.

"He seemed pretty tired. He'll probably sleep for
a while," she said.

"Good." Luke went into the kitchen and came
back with his hat. "Well, if he's going to sleep,

I'll…'' He paused with his hat halfway to his head. His gaze bounced up to meet hers. "I can't go out to work," he said. "I can't leave him alone."

Shannon nodded sympathetically. "Welcome to fatherhood."

With a frustrated growl, Luke clapped his hat onto the hat rack. "This isn't fatherhood," he said, whirling to her. "This is only temporary. No way is this going to be permanent."

"Well, no," she said carefully, taken aback by his vehemence. "You said your sister would be back for him."

"That's right." He took a couple of frustrated turns around the room. "Then things will get back to normal around here."

Meaning lonely, Shannon thought. Even though she knew she should drop the subject, she was compelled to ask, "Why, Luke, don't you ever have plans to be a father?"

"He—" He glanced toward the bedroom. "I mean, heck, no. I like being a bachelor. I like it fine." He stalked over and fell into his chair. "I'm just not cut out to be a husband or father."

Shannon's heart sank, but this was too interesting not to pursue it. She sat on the couch and leaned forward intently, propping her chin in her palm. "Mind telling me why not? I mean, most people want families."

He lifted an eyebrow at her. "*Family* is what got me to this place in Colorado instead of on my own ranch in Arizona." At the coldness in his voice and the no-trespassing expression on his face, Shannon sat back as abruptly as if he'd taken a swing at her.

She had better consider herself told, she thought, hurt. He was still pained by the betrayal of his stepmother and wasn't going to let anything begin to heal him. She felt sorry for him, not just because of what had been done to him, but because he was a strong man who could overcome it if he chose. Instead, he seemed to be content to live with one foot in the past, to hibernate and let the world pass by him.

"You may change your mind someday," she answered in a cool tone. Not willing to hear him deny that, she hurriedly stood. "I came out today to get my hat. Is it still in your truck?"

That snapped him out of his brooding. He straightened in his chair. "Yes, but you're not leaving, are you?"

"Well, *I* am supposed to be working today." She would have liked to fool herself into thinking that the sudden distress in his eyes was because he liked her company, but she knew it had more to do with Cody and his care than it did with her. "I can stop by later and see how you're getting along."

He sent her a grateful look. "Thanks. I'd appreciate that."

Shannon hesitated before making the next suggestion, because she didn't know how he would take it. "Also, I can call my sister Becca and see if she knows someone who can come out and help you with Cody."

He frowned. "Well, I don't know."

Shannon shook her head. "I understand you're reluctant to have anyone else on your place, but you have to think about what's best for that baby."

Luke thrust his jaw out. "I don't need you to tell

me—'' He paused and shrugged, then ran a hand over his face. ''Maybe I do.''

''I'll call Becca right now.'' Shannon headed for the kitchen and phoned her sister, who said she would call around to friends and family to see if she could find some help for Luke.

When Shannon hung up, Luke was standing in the kitchen looking around. There were dirty dishes piled in the sink, and the floor was gritty. ''I guess a house needs to be pretty clean for a baby, huh?''

Shannon tucked her tongue into her cheek at his nonplussed expression. ''Most people seem to think so,'' she admitted.

His mouth turned down. ''I'd better clean the place up since I'm stuck inside today, anyway.''

''That might be a good idea,'' she agreed, heading for the front door. ''I'll be on my way. I've got to go over to the Otero ranch. I'm helping them design a new irrigation system. I should be back here—'' she glanced at her watch as she opened the screen door and strolled out ''—by two. There's a convenience market near their place. Do you want me to pick up anything for you?''

She walked down the shallow steps, then glanced at Luke, who had come out to the porch. She saw that he had an odd expression on his face.

''What?'' she asked, self-consciously looking at herself to see if something was unbuttoned or untucked.

His gaze came up to meet her eyes. He tilted his head as if he was trying to catch a faint chord of music drifting on the summer breeze. Slowly, he shook his head. ''Nothing,'' he said, studying her face. ''Nothing. I, uh, don't need anything from the store. I'll see you later.''

Still, with that strange look on his face, he turned and went into the house.

A shiver of apprehension danced across Shannon's shoulders. She tried to shake it off as she got her hat from Luke's truck and prepared to leave for her day's work. As she started the agency truck, she couldn't help wondering what had been behind that look.

CHAPTER SIX

WHAT had that been about? Luke rubbed his knuckles across his chin as he tried to bring his scrambled thoughts into line. When Shannon had started to leave, had been telling him about her day, asking if she could pick up something for him at the store, he'd had a moment of déjà vu. It seemed as if they had stood like that before sometime in the past, said those same things. Or that they would do so sometime in the future.

Luke frowned. He was a hardheaded, practical man. He wasn't given to flights of imagination. In fact, his stepmother, Catherine, had said he *had* no imagination, which was one of the reasons he couldn't picture selling Willow Springs Ranch to the developers who had been panting after it for years.

Thinking of Willow Springs, of what he'd lost, brought the usual sick, sinking feeling in the pit of his stomach, but right behind it came the memory of Shannon's question about having a family. He'd wanted those things once, but for two years he hadn't been able to consider the thought with any pleasure.

A family was a unit that stood together no matter what. They helped each other, supported each other. They didn't scheme and connive and look for ways to get what they wanted to the detriment of the others.

One member wasn't supposed to sell the family business out from under the others.

Luke's quick anger faded, leaving him feeling drained. He wondered if hanging on to it was making him bitter, something he'd never wanted to be. Was it possible that his budding bitterness was what made him so tired? Kept him from getting this place in shape faster, hiring hands, accepting help?

Luke shook off that thought. Nah. Those things brought interference, which was the last thing he needed.

Luke walked to the kitchen and began searching out cleaning supplies. That moment when he'd watched Shannon leaving and felt as if he didn't want her to go had been a freak occurrence, just a fluke, the product of his worries about being left alone with his nephew. It didn't mean a thing. He plucked a bottle of pine cleaner from beneath the sink and began reading the instructions.

When Shannon arrived at the Crescent Ranch three hours later, she climbed the front steps with her arms full of things she'd picked up at the convenience store. It would be better if Luke didn't have to make an emergency run to the store, taking Cody with him. She had seen only one container of concentrated formula for the baby. She'd also bought a box of diapers. It looked as though Luke would be going through large numbers of them before he got the hang of changing them.

Juggling her packages, she raised her hand to rap lightly on the screen door, but when a loud wail and a crash erupted from the back of the house, she swung the door open and charged inside.

The smell of pine cleaner rocked her on her boot

heels. Gasping, she hurried into the living room, where she dumped her purchases on the sofa. The place gleamed, but the pine smell was overwhelming enough to make her eyes water.

She didn't know why she was surprised. She should have guessed that a man like Luke would take his housecleaning seriously.

Shannon ran to the bedroom, where she found Luke trying to dress the baby in a fresh outfit. The rest of the house may have been clean, but this room looked like an explosion in a laundry. Baby clothes were thrown around, and half a dozen clean but discarded diapers littered the floor, their torn edges testimony to the difficulty Luke was having diapering the boy.

He was sitting on the end of the bed, his booted feet stuck out before him, one toe hooked under the edge of the dresser. He must have kicked it, because the lamp had been knocked off and lay on the floor. Cody was on his uncle's lap crying piteously and flailing his arms and legs as Luke gingerly tried to subdue and aim the sleeve of Cody's pajamas at his arm as it swung by.

He looked up when Shannon entered, and his face flooded with gratitude. "There's got to be some trick to this," he panted. "I know how to string barbed wire fence without it breaking and snapping back on me. I know how to doctor a Brahman bull without getting kicked. I even know how to capture a rabid dog, but I can't do this." He finally got Cody's arm in the sleeve and tried to pull the one-piece outfit to his legs.

Shannon smiled softly as she bent to pick up the lamp and replace it on the dresser. "Well, it would help if you weren't going at it backward," she pointed out.

"Huh?"

He looked so distressed and puzzled she almost laughed. "You need to put his feet in first, then put his arms in the sleeves and pull the suit up to his shoulders."

"Oh."

"What happened to his other suit, anyway?"

"Spit up." He looked at the discarded pajama suit on the floor and grimaced.

"You did bathe him, didn't you?"

Luke's mouth dropped open. "Bathe him? He's been sleeping all day. What could he possibly have done to need a bath? It's not like he's worked up a sweat."

Shannon's eyes sparkled. "It helps keep him from getting a rash, and don't forget about the spit up."

Luke shuddered. "As if I could."

"Also, he needs a daily bath because there are other smelly things his little body could...produce."

Luke closed one eye and grimaced comically. "I get the picture."

Shannon laughed. She didn't mind at all seeing him at a loss. It made him seem much more human. "Come on. I'll show you how to bathe him." She dug through Cody's things until she found a bar of baby soap, then grabbed a towel from the bathroom and led the way to the kitchen and its freshly scrubbed sink.

"Roll up your sleeves," she advised. He did so as she ran warm water in the sink, undressed Cody, then handed him to Luke, who eyed the naked, squirming body dubiously.

"I don't suppose this is anything like dipping calves into tick dip, is it?" he asked hopefully. "Just a quick in and out?"

Shannon choked on her laughter. "Afraid not. Put him in the sink, and I'll show you what to do."

Gingerly, Luke lowered Cody into the water. Shannon stood beside him and leaned over to show him how to slip his left hand under Cody's shoulders and grip his upper left arm, supporting him and keeping his head out of the water, while bathing him with his right. After the first few awkward minutes, Luke got the hang of it and gave Shannon a smug look. "Piece of cake," he said.

"Uh-huh."

Luke rinsed Cody and lifted him so that they looked at each other eye to eye. "I can do this," he informed the infant.

Cody responded by squirting the front of Luke's shirt.

With a whoop of laughter, Shannon twirled the towel around Cody and whisked him away.

Luke had rocked back on his heels, plucked the shirt away from his chest and stared in horror at the wet spot. "Little ingrate," he muttered. "You did that on purpose."

"Sorry," Shannon said, laughing. "But he really can't control his bladder yet."

"Humph." Luke unsnapped his shirt, pulled it off and tossed it onto the floor. He grabbed the soap, washed his chest, then rinsed it by leaning over the sink. Drops of water flew onto the pale yellow curtains and over the white tile countertop as he scrubbed vigorously. He dried himself with a fistful of paper towels.

Watching all this, Shannon clutched Cody to her pounding heart and nearly melted into a puddle right beside the soiled shirt.

Oh, he was impressive, she thought, nearly on the point of hyperventilating. Muscles, sinew, brawn, raw power were words that flashed through her mind.

She was no stranger to men. She'd been around them all her life, father, uncles, cousins, ranch hands. Even now, the majority of the people she worked with were men, but, oh, no one looked like this one.

He turned to her with water drops still clinging to the dark hair that arrowed into the waistband of his jeans. His eyes flashed up to meet hers when he saw that she hadn't moved.

Shannon gulped air and turned shakily toward the bedroom. "We, uh, better get him dressed," she wheezed.

Luke didn't respond as he followed, which was just as well. She couldn't have answered coherently. She diapered Cody, then handed him to Luke, who had picked up the clean pajama suit. He shook it out, then held it up to look it over.

Disgruntled, he glanced up and caught the look on her face. "Don't laugh," he warned. "You know people usually have a couple of days to figure out this process while the baby's still in the hospital and they've got armies of nurses and other people around to help."

She crossed her arms over her chest and watched him. She had to give him credit for one thing—he didn't give up easily. He sat on the edge of the bed, laid Cody across his lap and slipped the suit on.

"You may not have an army of nurses, but there are any number of people who would be willing to help you out."

He was silent. He wouldn't ask until he absolutely had to. He changed the subject, nodding toward the discarded pajama suit on the floor. "That spit up smells toxic. Do you think it is? He got some on my leg. I'm hoping it doesn't burn through to the skin."

"No doubt it's because of the change from breast milk to formula. It'll take him a few days to get used to it. We'd better hope he doesn't get colic."

As she spoke, Shannon stepped forward and leaned over to help him do up the last few snaps.

"I'll bet you don't doctor that the same way you do colic in horses, do you?" he asked, looking up.

In that instant, Shannon realized he was on the same level as her breasts. Her hands went still, and Cody, who had been wiggling, grew still. In the sudden silence, Shannon could hear her breath being slowly squeezed from her lungs.

If Luke leaned forward the tiniest bit, he could touch her with his nose or his lips. She told herself to move, but she remained frozen in place. Her face grew hot, and the heat moved down to her throat, then her chest. Her breasts tingled. Something was happening to them, and she prayed that he wouldn't notice it.

His eyes came up to hers. "You shouldn't get so close," he said in a husky voice. "I don't exactly smell like a bed of roses."

No. He smelled like baby soap.

The tip of her tongue snaked out to dampen her bottom lip. "In fact, you smell like you have every other time I've seen you."

His gaze fastened on her mouth. "How's that?"

"Masculine," she breathed, and her lips quirked into a smile. "But now with piquant overtones of pine cleaner and baby soap."

He didn't answer her smile, but his eyes narrowed, watching her, drawing her in. Warmth radiated from him in steady waves. She remembered that, and she remembered, too, the way his mouth had felt on hers, how he had tasted. Her gaze dropped to his lips. She wanted to taste him again.

His hand came up, as did his lips, as if he wanted to capture and hold her for a second. She drew imperceptibly closer.

Cody chose that second to begin fussing again.

As if she had been snapped out of a hallucination, Shannon blinked and straightened away from Luke, who looked as dazed as she felt. Then his expression closed, shutting her out. She blinked and glanced around the room, wondering into which corner her common sense and self-preservation had fled.

"No," she finally said, recalling what they'd been discussing before that moment of insanity. She stepped away, putting several feet of space between them. "You don't treat colic in a baby like you do in a horse. I'm afraid that with a baby, it mostly involves walking the floor with them. I do have some help coming for you, though. I talked to Becca earlier, and she's lined someone up."

"Who?"

"Our great-aunt Katrina." Shannon glanced toward the window. "In fact, she should be here soon."

"Your great-aunt?"

"Don't worry, she's not a doddering maiden aunt. Far from it," Shannon murmured. "She's had kids, grandkids and now great-grandkids, and she loves babies. Besides, she was the only person available when Becca called around."

Luke stood, holding Cody against him. The baby stopped fussing and stuffed his fist into his mouth.

"I don't know about this. How old is this great-aunt of yours?"

Shannon shrugged and headed for the living room to retrieve her purchases and put them away. "She'd like everyone to think she's sixty, but she admits to seventy-one. However, my dad once told me her true age, so I know she's at least a decade older than that."

"This woman's in her eighties and you expect her to take care of an infant?" he asked, outraged as he stalked along behind her. "Why, that's cruel, and besides, I don't want to be responsible if she works herself so hard she collapses."

Shannon burst out laughing at that idea. "That's not something you have to worry about with Katrina. Why don't you reserve judgment until you meet her?" She nodded toward a rooster tail of dust coming up the long drive from the main highway. It was being kicked up by the wheels of a gold Mustang convertible driven by a lady wearing a shocking pink head scarf and rhinestone-studded sunglasses. "Here she comes now."

*   *   *

"Shame on you two," Mary Jane said, looking from Shannon to Becca and back. "Sending Katrina to that poor man. She's probably got him tied up in knots with all her flirting and innuendos."

"It'll be good for him," Shannon answered firmly as she helped herself to another of her mother's biscuits. She had stopped by on her way home to beg some dinner and found Becca visiting with her children. After reporting on the day's events, Shannon had tucked into the food her mom had prepared for dinner.

She swallowed and looked up with a grin. "You should have seen his face, though, when she skidded to a stop in a cloud of dust and stepped out of her car wearing a hot pink shorts outfit and sandals with matching polish on her toenails and her inch-long fingernails." She took another bite and smiled smugly, her dark blue eyes glowing. "I can just about guarantee they don't have anything in Arizona like our great-aunt Kat."

Mary Jane snickered. "You're probably right. By now, she's spoiled the baby rotten and has Luke halfway convinced he should consider becoming her fifth husband."

"Luke doesn't want to be anybody's husband," Shannon said, then glanced from her mother to her sister. "Or so he says," she finished lamely. "And he seems to want to be left alone. Or at least, he did. I guess that's changed now, what with the baby and all."

"Does he want to be a hermit?" Becca asked, frowning and exchanging a look with Mary Jane.

Shannon paused before answering. She could tell

her mother and sister the story behind Luke's arrival in the Tarrant Valley, but the story really wasn't hers to tell. Besides, she could tell by the looks on their faces that the more she said about him, the more they would think there was something between her and Luke when there wasn't.

Finally, she answered, "He does seem to like to be alone, work alone."

Becca gave her an odd look when she didn't elaborate but was distracted when her son, Jimmy, announced he was finished eating and was going out to play. He took a swipe at his mouth, threw down his napkin and made his escape with Becca calling after him to stay out of the corral.

While this was going on, Shannon sipped from her glass of iced tea and thought about what she'd just said. Maybe it wasn't true that Luke preferred to work alone. He'd let her work with him. She considered the day they'd mended the fence and the kiss that had occurred afterward. She had relived that kiss a hundred times since it happened.

He had told her he was a bastard, and she hadn't believed him because she had felt and sensed that he was troubled. Now she knew it wasn't true, because he'd been willing to help his sister, to take on the care of an infant when he knew nothing about babies.

She wondered if he felt guilty and responsible because he hadn't been able to stop his stepmother from selling their ranch. He hadn't been the only one to lose his home. His sister had lost hers, as well. The move from her home had been hard on Jeanette and thrown her into a life-style that she might not have chosen otherwise.

It seemed to Shannon that Luke was a man who wanted to do the right thing, but he thought he needed to be alone to do it. That thought made her heart ache. He had been more approachable today than she'd ever seen him, but when little Cody was gone, she thought Luke would return to his solitary ways.

And there would be no further reason for her to see him.

Her mother and sister stirred her out of her musings by talking about the upcoming festivities for the Fourth of July. As usual, a rodeo was planned, as well as a parade and a dance at the county park. Shannon's thoughts turned to Luke, thinking that he probably wouldn't attend and telling herself it wasn't really her business, even though she wished it was.

Her mother interrupted her thoughts by standing and asking, "Anybody want dessert? I've got ice cream." She strode to the freezer and threw it open while Becca removed dessert dishes from the cupboard.

Shannon smiled at the cozy scene, but she wondered again if anything like this would ever happen in Luke's house. She thought it was unlikely.

Shannon's phone was ringing when she arrived home. She dropped her purse and keys on the sofa as she came in the door and scooped the receiver up on the third ring.

"Hello?"

"Shannon?"

A thrill ran through her when she recognized Luke's voice, but she was alarmed to hear Cody wailing in the background. "Yes, Luke, what is it? Is Cody all right?"

"That depends," came the grave response. "Does colic consist of bouts of crying punctuated by bouts of screaming?" he asked in a tired voice.

"I'm afraid so."

"Well, what do I do about it?"

"Um, I'm not sure. Isn't Aunt Katrina still there?"

"No, she went home to get ready for a...date."

Shannon giggled. "Oh, Mr. Cruz, I suppose." Katrina was going out with Brittnie's grandfather-in-law.

"Yeah." Luke cleared his throat. "Although she said if I was looking for a relationship, she'd dump him in a minute."

Laughing, Shannon said, "Did you turn red when she said that?"

"Hell, yes, and I covered Cody's ears, too."

"She only said it to watch you blush. She loves being outrageous."

"She succeeded."

They fell silent for a second, then Luke asked, "About the colic? What do I do? He really seems to be suffering."

Shannon glanced around her apartment. She could spend a quiet evening tending her plants, watching television, reading a book. Or she could go help Luke take care of a fussy baby.

No contest.

"I'll talk to Becca and find out what to do, then I'll be right over."

"Oh, you don't have to—" He broke off when

Cody gave a particularly pitiful yell. "Thanks, Shannon. I'd appreciate it."

Shannon quickly said goodbye, then called her sister. Acting on Becca's advice, she stopped by the drugstore just before it closed and bought the items her sister had suggested, then hurried out to Crescent Ranch.

When she drove up, she saw that he'd moved the rocking chair to the front porch and was sitting with the baby, rocking slowly while Cody cried and squirmed. Light from the living room spilled out, illuminating the two of them. Shannon's heart caught and did a slow roll in her chest at the sight of the big, tough cowboy trying to soothe the fussy infant.

She got out of her car. He stood and watched her approach with an expression of gratitude.

"Here you go," she said, handing him the bag of items she'd bought, then took Cody from his arms. The change in position quieted the infant momentarily.

Luke set the bag on the chair and pulled out a hot water bottle and a six-pack of his favorite beer.

Holding them up, he turned to face her and said, "We're going to get him drunk?"

"No, silly, that's for you. Becca says it works wonders for distraught fathers—or uncles. The hot water bottle is for Cody. Go fill it with warm water, and I'll show you what Becca told me to do."

As he did, Shannon walked the length of the porch, humming to Cody, who had resumed his fussing. She knew he was in pain. The colic that was normal for a baby his age was made worse by an upset stomach caused by the change to the unfamiliar formula.

Luke was back in a few minutes with the hot water bottle in one hand. He looked ready for business. "Now what?" he asked.

"Now we pray this works," she said, sitting in the rocker. She laid the bottle across her lap, placed a light blanket over it and gently put Cody, tummy first, on top. Turning his head to the side, she popped a pacifier into his mouth and began patting his back. He quieted immediately, and Luke looked at her as if she'd performed a miracle.

"Well, I'll be dam—darned," he breathed. "It works."

"Becca told me a few other tricks, too, in case this one didn't work."

"We may need them." He leaned against the porch railing and crossed his arms. He stood with his chin down gazing at the two of them thoughtfully.

"Why are you looking at me like that?" she asked after several minutes of his silent regard.

"I don't know, exactly," he said slowly. "I suppose I'm just trying to figure out what your reason is for all this." His hand lifted in a vague motion, taking in the baby and the water bottle. She knew he also meant the help she'd given, the aunt she and Becca had recruited to care for Cody. "Don't get me wrong," he said gruffly. "I'm grateful." The words seemed to stick in his throat.

"But you want to know what it's going to cost you?" she asked, her tone sharper than she'd meant it to be. Hurt and disappointed in him, she dipped her head, the long dark hair she'd loosened from her braid falling forward to hide her face. "Believe it or not,

Luke, not everyone has an ulterior motive. I saw that you needed help, so I helped you.''

He was quiet for a long time. The only sound was the faint creak of the rocker as she slowly moved back and forth, patting Cody's back, thinking her distressed thoughts. What had she expected, after all? That he would suddenly change completely? Lose that cloak of suspicion that seemed to shroud him? That he would declare he was as attracted to her as she was—

Shannon's mind veered away from that thought. One kiss—okay, a few bone-melting, breath-robbing, toe-curling kisses—didn't amount to attraction, she reminded herself furiously. It was just chemistry. Proximity.

Insanity.

It wouldn't be repeated. Still, she resented his determination to keep her at arm's length, especially since she was helping him out.

She looked up. ''Don't you have some chores that need to be done?'' she asked in a coolly dismissive tone. ''I'll take care of Cody so you can work, then I've got to get home.''

Luke pushed away from the railing and lifted a hand, palm up, as if in apology for insulting her. Shannon looked away, ignoring him, and after a moment, he left the porch and headed for the barn.

She slumped in the rocker, letting her spine rest against the back. Well, that had effectively put a stop to the silly air castles she'd been building, not that she'd put a real face or form to them.

Shannon pushed her toes against the wooden porch boards and rocked harder.

She had better reconcile herself to the fact that Luke was willing to accept her help, but it was strictly on a businesslike basis. She wouldn't be surprised if he tried to pay her. Of course, if he did, he would find out that she could be just as tough as he could. She'd seen some branding irons in his barn. It might be necessary for her to wrap one around his head.

Pleased at that thought, she rocked faster.

He didn't want favors or friends because that meant that once the crisis was over, there would be an obligation for her to continue coming around.

Well, she had a news flash for him. While it might be true that he was the sexiest, smartest, most attractive male challenge that had ever come her way, he was also stubborn and so impossibly suspicious that he would look a gift horse in the mouth. Who needed a man like that? Certainly not Shannon Kelleher— and that was a promise he could take to the bank!

When Cody dropped his pacifier and let out a wail, Shannon realized she'd been rocking them so furiously the chair had moved several inches across the floor. "Sorry, Cody," she muttered.

She carried him inside, washed his pacifier, changed his diaper and laid him in his crib. In spite of her irritation with Luke, she was pleased to see that he had moved the portable crib into his own bedroom, where he could have the baby close during the night.

She placed Cody on his back, where, exhausted from his bout of colic, he fell immediately to sleep. She covered him with a blanket and straightened to glance around the room.

For a man who claimed to want to be left alone in

his home, he wasn't making much of an effort to make his home comfortable and inviting. His bedroom was stark and utilitarian with only a double bed, which she thought was probably too short for him, a nightstand and a dresser. The only personal touch was a book lying facedown on the nightstand as if he'd been reading in bed before going to sleep.

Shannon picked up the book and took a peek at the title. She blinked in astonishment when she saw it was a work on Colorado range management. She was familiar with the author and had found his conclusions and suggestions worthwhile.

"Is he asleep?" Luke asked from behind her.

Startled, she turned with the book in her hand. "Yes," she whispered. "I think he'll sleep for a while.' Quickly, she replaced the volume on the nightstand and turned to leave the room. "Interesting reading," she commented as he stepped back to let her through the door.

He lifted an eyebrow at her. "I told you I'd take care of this place myself."

"Yes, you did. But you're going about it the hard way."

"I usually do."

"Because you think it's wise, or because you're just being stubborn?" She threw the question out and knew she should regret it, but she didn't. She was tired. Exhausted, in fact, and mentally bruised from the day's events.

"I told you how things were."

"Yes, you did." She nodded. "But things change. People change."

He narrowed his eyes. "Except me."

"So it seems."

He didn't like that. When she started to walk around him, he stepped in front of her and flattened his hand against the wall. She rocked to a stop, her nose a millimeter from the inside of his elbow. Her gaze swept up to meet his.

He was frowning. "Shannon, I appreciate all you've done. All you're doing—for me and for Cody." He tilted his head toward the porch. "What I said out there, well, I didn't mean it like it sounded."

Her fury melted away, leaving only sadness. She lifted her hand and rested her palm along his jaw. Surprise jumped in his eyes, followed by a spark of heat. She felt the muscle in his jaw flex beneath her palm.

"Yes, you did, Luke," she answered solemnly. "And that's what's so sad." His arm lifted as if he was going to reach for her, but she dropped her hand, ducked beneath his elbow and headed for the door. "Give me another call if you need anything. Otherwise, you're at Great-Aunt Kat's mercy. Have fun," she said with a breeziness she didn't feel.

She thought her getaway would be quick, clean, but he had other ideas. Two steps down the hall, she was pulled up short by his hand on her elbow. He spun her around. His eyes seared into hers.

"You're so sure of yourself, so sure you have all the answers, know what's right for everyone else."

"No, I'm not," she answered furiously, trying to shrug him off.

But his hands, big, rough, warm, captured her shoulders. "Maybe not," he said in a low, angry voice. "But you at least think you've got me all figured out. Know what's best for me."

"No." Her heart started beating in her throat. Fear, excitement, she didn't know what it was. Adrenaline surged through her bloodstream.

He drew her forward. She stumbled against his chest and put her hands up to stop herself. It was like hitting a steel curtain, but warm, vital. She felt his muscles bunch and shift beneath her palms. Her fingers flexed. She wanted to move away, but for some reason, she stayed.

"Why is that, Shannon?" His voice had gone low, silky. "Do you spend a lot of time thinking about me? About what would be best for me?"

"Cert—certainly not," she stammered. Her arms as stiff as fence posts, she tried to hold him off, but he was stronger than she was, and he pulled her closer.

"I think you do, Shannon." He lowered his head and ran his nose along one of her twisting curls, then flicked his tongue over her earlobe.

Desire exploded in her like a bomb, shuddering upward in devastating waves. "No," she breathed.

"I spend a lot of time thinking about what would be best for you, Shannon, and I think this is it."

She knew what he was going to do. She knew she should fight him off, demand that he let her go. She also knew she would do neither one. Instead, she turned her head to where his lips were plucking at her ear and captured them with her own.

From Luke's throat came a low, satisfied sound as if this was what he'd been prodding her to do and he approved that she'd finally caught on. He pulled her closer, deepening the kiss, though Shannon's hazy brain couldn't think how it could get much deeper. She opened to him, reveling in the heat he generated within her, recalling how it had been before when they'd nearly made love in the back of his truck, right there in the outdoors, with the sun beating down on them.

Shannon's arms gave up the fight to hold him off. She slid them around his neck, plunging her fingers greedily into his hair. He lifted her up so she had to scramble for a foothold, finally resting her toes precariously on the tops of his boots.

She should have felt wobbly, unsure, but instead, with her feet off the floor and all her senses fully involved in kissing him, she felt as if she'd taken a step over some boundary, trusted him to know what was best for her. That thought finally connected with what he'd just said. He was trying to prove something, maybe that he was the one in control, that she could go only so far and no farther, that he'd accept her help, even ask for it, but only on his terms. That was one-sided and unfair and compelled Shannon to drag her mouth away. At last, her common sense returned. She pulled out of his arms and stumbled away.

He started to protest, and his hands came up to bring her back to him, but when he saw the dismay in her eyes, the way the back of her hand came up to cover her swollen, aching lips, his arms fell to his sides. Regret flickered in his eyes, then all expression drained from them as he looked at her.

"No," she said shakily. "That isn't what's best for either of us. It complicates things—"

"Yes," he interrupted. "It does." He stepped back, making way for her to pass. "You'd better go."

Blindly, she rushed past him, left the house and hurried to her car. She wasn't falling in love with him. She *wasn't*. He suspected her of secret motives. As she jabbed the key toward the ignition, tears filled her eyes. She thought of how she had been so careful while dressing that morning, and guilt pricked her conscience.

Maybe she did have a secret motive, but it wasn't the one he suspected. In spite of all she'd done, he thought the worst of her. How could she love a man like that?

She started the car and turned it in a slow circle in the drive. As she passed the house, she saw him silhouetted in the doorway, watching her leave. She turned her head away.

She didn't love him. That was the answer. She couldn't. So why did it feel as if she'd left a chunk of her heart behind?

CHAPTER SEVEN

LUKE didn't call, so she concluded he didn't need anything more from her. Shannon was so shaken up by their last encounter that she didn't want to hear from him. She wanted to know how Cody was adjusting, though, so she called Great-aunt Katrina, who reported that Cody was doing fine, that his parents were expected back any day now and that his colic was better.

For the next week, Shannon kept herself very busy. It seemed that Wiley had many projects and problems for her to solve. She didn't mind too much, because she was occupied, and her thoughts were off of Luke.

All of this was going through her mind a few days later when she happened to be in her small office doing paperwork. She preferred being out in the field, but this was a necessary part of her job. She started in surprise as Wiley entered without knocking.

She couldn't help the irritation that crossed her face, but she masked it quickly and greeted him in a cool tone. "I'm sorry, Wiley, I was so involved in what I was doing that I didn't hear you knock."

They both knew he hadn't knocked, but his lips curled in a smile that showed his teeth. Shannon had always thought his teeth resembled his office—brown around the edges. Grimacing at the unpalatable image, she met his eyes. He'd seen the look she'd given him, and he didn't like it, but she knew he didn't care enough to turn around and leave her to her work.

"That's okay, Shannon. I just wanted to bring your mail in."

She blinked. They had a secretary who sorted their mail and delivered it. "Did Linda go home sick?" she asked, taking the stack from him. He didn't let go right away, forcing her to meet his eyes. She saw a smile that sent slivers of apprehension through her.

Wiley finally released the letters. "Nah, but I told her I'd do it. I wanted to talk to you, anyway." To her alarm, he turned and closed the door behind him.

Shannon stood to face him across her desk. When he wanted to talk to her, he called her into his office. He rarely entered hers, and she didn't like having him here. Her voice was unwelcoming as she asked, "What did you need to talk to me about?"

"Your work performance, for one thing."

Immediately incensed, Shannon pointed to the stack of reports she'd just finished writing. "There's nothing wrong with my work performance."

He narrowed his eyes. "Everyone could stand some improvement in their work."

Especially you, she thought, but she kept silent and waited for him to go on.

He cleared his throat. "Ah, well, anyway, I thought we could get together and talk about it."

"I thought that's what you were doing right now, though you haven't actually said what it is about my work you object to." Aggressively, she put her hands on her hips and waited. If he didn't get to the point soon, she might have to pick him up and toss him out. That idea cheered her considerably.

"I mean, we can get together away from here and discuss it. Go out for a drink."

She stared at him. He was asking her out! She knew he'd begun dating since his wife had left and filed for divorce, but surely he didn't see her as a possible date. They couldn't stand each other. On the other hand, a change in his attitude toward her had occurred about the time his wife had left. Wiley hadn't liked her before. Then he'd become preoccupied with her. Maybe even obsessed.

"I don't think that would be a good idea," she said, knowing her distress was obvious in her voice. "We need to keep things...our business relationship strictly that. Business. Whatever you need to say to me, you can say here."

Anger flared in his eyes, and he placed his hands on her desk, leaned across it and glared at her. Shannon barely kept herself from recoiling in disgust.

"Who are you saving it for, Shannon? That cowboy you've been seeing out at the Crescent Ranch?" he asked, sneering. "I hear you been spending a lot of time out there. Are you putting out for him? What makes him so much better than me?"

Millions of things! Shannon's horror began to abate, and she grew angry. "My personal life is none of your business. What you're suggesting to me is sexual harassment."

He straightened. "You'd have to prove it first, wouldn't you?" He turned to go. "Your word against mine, honey," he said, his gaze raking her one last time. "Your word against mine."

Wiley walked out and closed the door with a snap. Shannon sank into her chair and pressed her hands to her lips. She'd frequently been on the receiving end of teasing smirks and remarks, but she'd never before been so blatantly propositioned. And by Wiley Frost, of all people. She didn't know quite what to do, though a thousand ideas were flying through her head, most of them violent.

She was certain about one thing. She was never again going to be alone with him. If he tried to shut the two of them in her office again, she would get up and walk to Linda's desk. If he had business to discuss, he could do it there.

After a few deep breaths, Shannon felt calmer, but she couldn't understand what had prompted this. She knew the cowboy he mentioned referred to was Luke. Little did he know she *had* no relationship with Luke. She wouldn't tell Wiley that, though, because he wouldn't believe her, and it was none of his business, anyway.

Disturbed, Shannon forced her mind back to her work, determined to do her best on the paperwork and avoid any further discussions of her job performance.

She was still distressed hours later when she arrived home. The apartment was stuffy, so she turned on the air conditioner and changed into the red shorts and top outfit Brittnie had given her. She poured herself some iced tea and downed two glasses while she gazed into the refrigerator and tried to decide what she would like to eat. Sandwiches again, she decided, though she thought the encounter with Wiley might have permanently impaired her appetite.

She was pulling out bread, sliced turkey and lettuce when she heard a knock on the door. She reached for the knob, then hesitated, thinking it might be Wiley.

She shook her head. Surely he wouldn't be that stupid. She swung the door open and was startled to see Luke standing there, holding Cody.

Luke's eyes swept over her from her long, tanned legs to the wavy black hair she'd loosened from her braid and brushed out. He took off his hat and nodded toward the baby in the crook of his arm. "Cody told me I needed to come apologize."

Shannon stared at the man standing in her doorway. Luke had come to apologize? She met his eyes, and he gave a rueful shrug as if he couldn't understand it, either.

"I asked Katrina where you lived," he explained. He took in the waist-length black hair that rippled, loose and free, over her back and shoulders, the bright red shorts outfit, her bare feet and the red polish she'd daringly, and uncharacteristically, used on her toenails. His lips twitched when he saw that.

"I'm glad you did." Happiness flooded through her, shone from her eyes. It took her a moment to gather her wits enough to step back, swing the door wide and say, "Come in."

As she let him in, she reached to take Cody from him. He smelled sweet and clean, and his dark blue eyes met hers seriously. "Oh, I think he's grown," she said, cuddling him.

"He does feel heavier, doesn't he?" Luke asked, stepping inside and removing his hat. Shannon sensed a hint of pride in his voice as if he was pleased with himself for taking good care of his nephew.

Luke glanced around as if looking for a place to hang his hat, a black Stetson with a band of small silver conchas around the brim. Shannon pointed to the row of hooks she'd attached to a board and hung on the wall. Giddy with joy, Shannon wanted to tell him that he could hang his hat in her house anytime, then felt herself blush with embarrassment at the trite phrase.

"Heavier and more handsome," Shannon agreed, smiling into Cody's curious eyes. She was glad to see that he was dressed in an outfit appropriate for the evening, which was supposed to turn cool. His diaper didn't sag, either, which told her that Luke had mastered that trick.

"We were wondering if you'd like to go for a walk with us."

She looked up from examining Cody and gave Luke a skeptical frown. "After working all day, you came all the way into town to go for a walk?"

"Sounds lame, doesn't it?" He shrugged again, as if admitting she'd caught him. "Truthfully, I wanted to say I'm sorry because I acted like a jackass the other night and to see if you'd like to go get something to eat with us. I'm tired of eating my own cooking, and Cody's tired of my company, though I admit he's pretty enthralled with Katrina. He wouldn't mind if she stuck around all the time."

"Most men are enthralled with Katrina. I think she has some kind of magical powers that attract them. Or maybe she's just a shameless flirt," Shannon added with a laugh.

"You've got that right," he answered sardonically.

How susceptible was Luke to Katrina's flirting? True, Katrina was so good-natured and so apprecia-tive of men, they were usually flattered by her attention, no matter what their age, but they didn't take her seriously, as Luke obviously didn't.

What if she tried a little of it herself, Shannon thought. After all, the apple didn't fall far from the tree, and she had picked up a few tips from Katrina over the years.

Shannon knew she should feel ashamed for entertaining those thoughts. She had worked hard to avoid the stereotypical behavior people often expected of her because of her looks. She wasn't a hypocrite who would suddenly start using feminine wiles to get her way, but still, a little flirting might be interesting.

The best part was that her family, friends and colleagues would be stunned. She had never been a flirt, no matter what Wiley Frost might think.

She glanced at Luke, who was examining her apartment with interest, taking in the cheerful colors, the slightly frayed furniture, the plants that exploded from every imaginable type of container. He was looking the place over as if he was trying to gain some insight into her character, but she knew his interest could turn to cool reserve, even disdain, in a flash.

Flirting could wait. Perhaps she was a coward, but she wasn't willing to risk this fragile peace between them.

Luke turned to her. "Nice place," he said. "It looks comfortable. Homey." He shrugged as if to acknowledge that they both knew his place wasn't and never would be. "So, how about it? Are you willing to go out with a couple of guys, one who cries and spits up sometimes and one who acts like a jackass most of the time?"

Shannon didn't even have to give it a moment's

thought. "I'd love to," she said. "I guess you know there aren't many places to eat here in Tarrant, though Joe's Diner has great barbecue and it's just around the corner."

"We'll go there, then."

She handed Cody to him. "Sit down while I get my sandals." She hurried to her bedroom, got her sandals, and also freshened her makeup and sprayed on her favorite perfume, probably wildly inappropriate for eating barbecue at Joe's Diner, but she didn't care.

When she rejoined Luke and Cody, he gave her a look as if he knew what she'd been doing and was pleased. She wondered how long it had been since a woman had tried to make herself attractive for him. As they left the apartment, he reached for his hat, then paused.

"Maybe I'll leave it here, if you don't mind," he said. "I don't like hanging it where someone might grab it at a restaurant, and it crowds the table if I put it there."

"Most men leave theirs on rather than risk having them stolen in a public place," Shannon pointed out as she locked the door and pocketed the key.

"But my mama raised me to take off my hat inside," Luke answered as if that was the last word on the subject.

Shannon smiled and led the way out to the parking lot. They stopped by Luke's truck to get Cody's stroller and diaper bag, then wandered down the sidewalk side by side, Luke pushing the baby.

Shannon gave him a sidelong glance, struck by the incongruity of Luke's cattleman's hands wrapped around the handles of the stroller. He didn't appear to be the least bit self-conscious. That didn't surprise her. She'd already figured out that he didn't much care what other people thought.

She felt a flutter in the region of her heart and knew she was very close to falling in love with him.

When they reached Joe's Diner, they saw that it was bustling, as usual. They managed to find a table in the corner and a place to park the stroller out of the flow of traffic. Shannon was amused to see Cody drop off to sleep in spite of the noise and the singer on the stereo system lamenting a lost love.

They ordered baskets with barbecued beef sandwiches and French fries, even though Shannon knew from experience that the meal would contain more calories than she usually ate in a day. When she said as much to Luke, he responded, ''I didn't think you were the kind of woman who worried about that.''

''Every woman does,'' she answered, swirling a French fry in catsup and popping it into her mouth. ''I'm no different.''

''Oh, yes, you are.'' He said it with a mixture of humor and puzzlement that made her toss her head and laugh. As she did so, she glanced across the room and caught sight of someone she knew. It happened all the time at Joe's, but she rarely met anyone looking at her with such venom.

Wiley Frost sat alone at a table. His eyes were fixed on her in a deadly glare.

Shannon choked on her French fry and started to cough.

''Hey, are you all right?'' Luke was on his feet

instantly, ready to pound her on the back or perform the Heimlich.

She waved him away. "I'm okay," she gasped. "It just went down the wrong way." With a watery smile, she reached for her glass of soda and took a sip. Luke clasped her shoulder with a brief, warm touch and resumed his seat.

Another quick glance across the room told her that Wiley had seen that solicitous gesture. She sighed inwardly. She knew she would pay for that tomorrow. Oh, why had Wiley complicated their already unpleasant working relationship by deciding they needed to have a personal one, as well?

"Are you sure you're all right?" Luke asked, his eyes searching her face.

She nodded, shoving aside her worries about Wiley and focusing on the man she was with, the only one she wanted to be with. "I'm fine. Truly. I shouldn't try to laugh and swallow at the same time." She took another careful sip of her drink and asked, "What have you heard from your sister? How's Cody's father?"

"He's better. Turns out he had some broken ribs and a concussion, but she thinks he'll be able to travel in a few days so they'll be coming to get Cody." Luke glanced automatically to check on his nephew. "Steve's going to give up the rodeo, though they don't know what he'll do yet." He took a bite of his sandwich and chewed thoughtfully.

It was on the tip of Shannon's tongue to suggest he offer the young man a job, though she knew he'd disdain the idea. After all, he'd told her more than once that he liked to work *alone*. Before she could speak, there was a rush of bodies beside their table, and she looked up to see her cousins, Ben and Tim Sills, and their girlfriends.

"Hey, Shannon," Ben said, grinning and eyeing Luke good-naturedly. "This the new boyfriend?" His eyes widened when he glanced across the table and saw Cody asleep in his stroller. He leaned across to inspect the sleeping infant, then looked at his cousin in awe. "Uh, Shannon, you been up to something we don't know about?"

Shannon felt an unaccustomed blush climbing her cheeks. "Hello, Ben," she answered, sending him dagger looks while she put one hand in the middle of his chest to shove him back. "Actually, I've been up to lots of things you probably don't know about." She nodded across the table to her companion. "This is Luke Farraday. And that's his nephew, Cody. Luke, these are my cousins, Ben and Tim Sills."

Luke rose, the solid set of his shoulders telling Shannon he was ready for some kind of confrontation. She could have told him he didn't have to worry, but Tim saved her the trouble by grinning widely, elbowing his brother aside and sticking his hand out to Luke.

"You're the guy who bought the Crescent Ranch out from under us. Man, I wish I knew why old Gus Blackhawk is such a son of a—" Shannon cleared her throat, and he laughed "—gun. Oh, well, if we'd bought it we would have been up to our necks in hock for the rest of our lives. I hear you paid cash. Must have shocked old Gus right out of his long underwear."

Shannon sent Luke a quick look. She didn't know

he'd paid cash outright for the place. Maybe he didn't
need the grant money he could get by joining the
conservation project. Or maybe he had spent all his
capital in buying the ranch and did need the grant
money but was so stubborn, proud or determined to
depend only on himself that he refused to accept help.

Her cousins were grinning hugely and so full of
good nature and fun that Luke was taken aback. He
scanned their faces, then nodded and said, "Yeah,
Mr. Blackhawk seemed a little shocked. Haven't seen
much of him since, so I don't know if he recovered
from it or not."

"Nobody sees much of Gus," Ben said. "He keeps
to himself, and that's fine with the rest of us."

"Ben," Shannon warned, her eyes scanning the
room. Like any other small town, Tarrant had a main
occupation—gossip. Her parents had raised her and
her sisters by the precept that no matter how nasty
Mr. Blackhawk became, they didn't retaliate, and they
didn't talk about him outside the family.

Ben winked at her. He and Tim introduced their
girlfriends, who said hello, giggled and drew their es-
corts to a table of their own.

Luke slowly resumed his seat. "Looks like they're
not holding a grudge."

"Why bother?" Shannon asked, taking a sip of her
soda. "Holding grudges is a waste of time and en-
ergy." When his eyes lanced to hers, she pinched her
lips and looked away. The unspoken observation that
he very possibly was holding a grudge against his
stepmother was as plain between them as footprints
in dried mud. She cleared her throat. "However,
that's just my humble opinion." Treating him to a

bright smile, she pushed the last of her food away, then saw that Cody was waking from his nap. "I'm finished," she announced. "How about you?"

He didn't answer for a minute, then one side of his mouth curved in a small smile. "I take back what I said the day we met."

She raised an eyebrow at him. "You said a great many things that day, Luke. Which one do you mean?"

"The one about you not having the whole diplomacy thing down very well. You seem to be getting the hang of it."

She wrinkled her nose at him as she stood. "I'm so glad you approve."

That brought a laugh from him, and across the room, she saw Wiley's head come up. He gave her another dark look, then returned to his meal, pointedly ignoring her. Secretly, Shannon couldn't have been happier, but she knew this wasn't the end of it.

While Luke paid their bill, she took Cody into the ladies' room and changed his diaper. He looked around curiously as he chewed on his fist. "I hope that when your parents come to pick you up, they stay for a while," she whispered. "I'm going to miss you. So is Katrina, and your uncle Luke is *really* going to miss you, though he probably wouldn't admit it."

She considered the changes she'd seen in Luke since they had met. Five minutes after meeting her, he'd been ready to throw her off his place. He wanted nothing more than to be left alone and he wanted nothing to do with his family, or anyone else, for that matter. Now he was taking care of his nephew and seeking her out for a meal together.

She picked the baby up and glanced in the mirror. Her face was flushed with pleasure, her eyes shining. She was a walking advertisement of how wonderful she thought it was to be in Luke's company. She knew that was what Wiley had seen in her face, and that was why he was angry with her.

"Well," she said to Cody. "That's his problem." But she knew it wasn't. At some point she would have to talk to Wiley about it. She dreaded that, but she wasn't going to let it spoil her evening.

She rejoined Luke and they walked outside together. She placed Cody in his stroller as Luke nodded toward the diner. "That was your boss in there, wasn't it?"

Startled, she looked up, wondering if he had picked up on her thoughts. "Uh, yes."

Wiley came out of the diner, gave Shannon a sweeping, dismissive glance and started in the other direction.

"Doesn't look like a happy man," Luke said, watching Wiley's short, rapid strides.

"He's not."

Luke considered her as if he wanted to ask more, but she turned away to rummage through the diaper bag. "Is Cody going to be hungry soon? If so, we could get Joe to warm his bottle and we could go sit in the park while we feed him."

When he didn't answer, she glanced up. "Luke?"

He was watching Wiley drive away, his eyes narrowed in thought. He didn't hear her until she called his name again. "What? Oh, oh, yeah. Cody'll be hungry. The park sounds fine."

She started inside to ask Joe to warm up Cody's

bottle, but Luke stopped her by laying his hand on her arm. "Has that guy been bothering you?"

Her start of surprise seemed to be all the answer he needed. "He has, hasn't he? I thought so."

"It's nothing serious, Luke." She hoped. She gave him a teasing grin. "Besides, aren't you the guy who wants to be left alone, not get involved in the community?"

"This isn't a community problem," he said in a hard tone. "It's a personal problem, and I'm not going to stand by and let some jerk hit on my g—uh, friend."

Goose bumps ran over Shannon in waves. Had he been about to say *girl?* She caught the frostiness in his eyes. Probably not, she thought with an inward sigh, but hey, at least he was willing to admit they were friends. "That's nice of you, Luke, truly, but it's nothing." She wondered hysterically when Luke had become "nice."

He didn't seem to like having that word tagged to him, either. "I don't like the way he looks at you," he said.

Her jaw dropped. "How does he look at me?" She knew, but she wanted to know how Luke saw it.

"Like he owns you. Or wants to."

Shannon gulped. She couldn't think of anything to say. "I...I can handle it, Luke. Don't worry about it." She brushed past him and went inside the diner to have Cody's bottle warmed, her mind in a confusion of worry about Wiley, amazement at Luke's reaction to Wiley and dashed hopes because Luke didn't seem to see her the way she wanted him to.

Admittedly, she wasn't exactly sure what way that was.

She had to let this rest. The evening had been so promising when they had started out. She wanted it to stay that way, but in some subtle manner, things had changed.

It was no good for her to worry over it like a dog with a bone. With a smile, Shannon thanked the waitress for warming the bottle, waved to her cousins and returned to Luke and Cody.

She didn't know what she was going to do about Wiley, but she wasn't ready to discuss it. Instead, she pointed to the plate glass window of Montoya's grocery store, which was plastered with posters announcing the Fourth of July celebrations.

"If you come to that, you can meet more of your neighbors," she advised him, determined to change the subject. They crossed the street to the small city park, dodging running children and teenagers playing Frisbee. They found an empty picnic table and sat down. Shannon happily cuddled Cody and began giving him his bottle.

Luke stretched his legs out in front of him, leaned back with his elbows on the table, and tilted his head. He was the picture of relaxation. "And if I don't want to meet more of my neighbors?"

Shannon gave him a swift glance, but she saw that he had a glint in his eyes. Her own rounded in surprise. "Are you teasing me? I never would have thought you were capable of it. It seems so—so..."

"Human?" he supplied, not insulted by her baiting of him. "I've been known to act human on occasion."

The way he kissed flashed through her mind. Oh, yeah, he could act human on a *very* elemental level. She breathed deeply to steady the sudden fluttering in her heart and looked at Cody. The baby had his tiny fists against his chest as he concentrated on draining his bottle. She smiled at his intensity, and her mind drifted to the way Luke kissed. He had that same intensity. What kind of hopeless nut case was she to compare a baby drinking his bottle to Luke's kisses? She veered to their conversation.

"If you don't come to the festivities on the fourth, it'll be your loss."

"No doubt." He tilted his head. "You're determined to drag me kicking and screaming into the life of this community, aren't you?"

"Maybe," she said noncommittally. The truth was that she had somehow become convinced she was the one who should drag him kicking and screaming into *life*. Perhaps what Luke had said was right—she had him all figured out and knew what was best for him, or at least thought she did.

"I have to wonder why you care."

"Because I..." She realized she'd been about to say, "love you." No, that was impossible. She didn't love him. She'd thought this out very carefully and decided she couldn't love someone who suspected her motives. She couldn't. She didn't even know him, and what she did know she sometimes didn't like. The park and the street beyond seemed to spin before her eyes, the sidewalk, cars, trees, people whirling around her in a dizzying dance. She jerked, pulling the bottle's nipple from Cody's hungry mouth. He let out a wail.

Alarmed, Luke sat up and turned to her. "Hey, are you okay? Did you get bit by something? There are some mosquitoes out, and…"

"No," she said, shakily settling Cody and returning the nipple to his mouth. "Sorry, little guy," she whispered.

"You're not dizzy again, are you? Damn." He cursed under his breath. "I thought you said you were over that ear infection."

She answered with a hollow laugh. "I'm fine. I just wasn't… Sorry." She looked down. "And Cody's okay."

For a moment, she didn't think Luke was going to accept that, but he nodded and said, "You want me to take over with him? I didn't mean to dump him on you. After all, he's my responsibility."

"No. I'm happy to do this. I haven't seen him all week."

A heavy silence stretched between them. She hadn't been to see Cody because she'd been hurt by Luke's treatment. He clenched his jaw and sat forward, his hands hanging loosely between his knees, but he didn't respond.

Shannon was just as happy he didn't. After all, he'd already apologized. What more could he say?

She couldn't worry about his thoughts. She needed to concentrate on her own. She felt as if a load of bricks had dropped on her. She was flattened, broken, unable to move.

She couldn't be in love with Luke Farraday. She'd known him less than a month. This wasn't how it happened, was it? She couldn't love someone who very often didn't even seem to like her. Her mind scrambled like little mice feet running on a wheel. He was barely ready to admit that they could be friends while her treacherous heart was leaping ahead and diving, eyes tight shut, nose pinched, into love.

It was impossible. She couldn't think about it. She concentrated on feeding Cody, burping him and returning him to his stroller for the trip to her apartment. Luke gave her a number of curious looks, but the conversation had somehow died between them, and neither of them tried to resurrect it.

"He's all set," Shannon said with forced brightness and a smile brittle enough to shatter.

Luke stood, looked at her with puzzlement and lifted his hand in an oddly touching gesture, then he seemed to see the dazed stiffness in her face. With a swift nod and another curious look, he said, "Maybe we'd better get you home."

"Yes." Her voice was as dull as her brain. "I'm tired." Pushing Cody's stroller, she walked swiftly from the park.

Within a few minutes, they rounded the block to her apartment building. "I'll leave you here," she said when they arrived at the parking lot. At his truck, which was parked beneath a lamppost, she turned and smiled, though her lips felt wooden. "You don't need to see me to the door. Thanks for dinner. It was a great apology." She wanted to get away from him, to think over this shattering discovery.

"All right," he said, his face puzzled. "I'll see you, then."

"Yes, of course." Her gaze darted around the parking lot, looking everywhere but at him. She bent to give Cody a goodbye pat, then gave a laugh that came off sounding pitiful. "I'll be seeing you around, especially if you decide to come out of hibernation and become part of the community."

He didn't respond, his eyes watching her nervous flutterings. Knowing he was probably speculating that she'd suddenly lost her mind, Shannon was sorry, but she could only concentrate on getting away from him. She thought about shaking his hand, giving him an impersonal kiss on the cheek, but she knew she would degenerate into a babbling fool if she touched him.

She almost laughed. She was already a fool in her own eyes. There was no need to compound things.

Finally, she fluttered her fingers at him and said, "Well, good night, then." She turned and fled, her heels beating a staccato rhythm on the asphalt.

CHAPTER EIGHT

WHAT the hell? Luke watched Shannon dash across the parking lot as if he'd suddenly turned into the village kidnapper. She couldn't wait to get away from him. He shook his head and reached up to push back his hat, only to discover his hat wasn't there. He'd left it in her apartment. Well, he'd be darned if he was going to go ask for it. She was so skittish, she might run across the living room and leap out the window to get away from him.

"I don't get it, Cody. What did I say? What did I do?"

Cody didn't seem to know, either. He waved his hands around and made gurgling sounds.

"You're no help, buddy. Don't you know we men are supposed to stick together when it comes to figuring out women?" Luke bent to scoop the baby out of the stroller and into his car seat. After buckling him in securely, he placed Cody's equipment in the truck, climbed in and started toward home. All the while, his mind was replaying the evening.

Everything had seemed fine. He wouldn't have blamed her if she'd shut the door in his face when he'd shown up, baby in hand and hangdog expression on his face. She hadn't, though. She'd seemed glad to see him, thrilled to see Cody, willing to spend the evening with him. What had gone wrong?

Should he have objected when she pitched right in

135

and started looking after Cody? It hadn't occurred to him, because he already knew that was her way. She wasn't the kind of woman who waited to be asked. She did whatever needed to be done.

He leaned his arm on the windowsill and ran his thumb over his chin. No, it wasn't caring for Cody that had caused the sudden change in her.

He reconstructed the evening, their conversation, meeting her cousins, seeing her boss glaring at them from across the room. Luke had recognized that look. It didn't take a genius to see the man was jealous. Had Shannon felt guilty about being with Luke? Nah. She'd made it clear she couldn't stand her boss. Luke wondered if she knew her boss didn't feel the same way about her. Probably.

Luke shifted on the seat, glanced in the rearview mirror, then resumed his thinking. It was disconcerting to recall his stab of elemental jealousy, the deepest and strongest emotion he'd let himself feel in months. Had Shannon seen it and been scared off by it?

No. She wasn't the type of woman who would run from that, might even have been flattered by it. Was it possible she'd become bored with their conversation, wanted to be rid of him?

Carefully, he went over what they'd been talking about when that strange look had passed over her face. It had been about him becoming part of the community, meeting his neighbors.

Luke frowned, slowed to make the turn into his ranch and drove toward the empty house, symbol of his solitary life. He stopped the truck and sat staring at the cottage. Had Shannon suddenly realized that he was a hopeless case? That she shouldn't waste her time with him?

He didn't like that conclusion at all. With a jolt that traveled through him with the force of an electric shock, he realized that he cared what she thought, didn't want her to give up on him.

When had that happened? And how had it happened without him seeing it coming? He didn't want to feel it. He wanted to go on as he'd been since his father had died, holding on to the anger that drove him, putting other, more positive emotions on hold.

He was determined to keep on that way. It saved time and trouble.

Luke looked at his innocent nephew. Against his will, he felt himself soften. He reached a finger out to Cody, who clasped it in a grip that went straight to Luke's heart. Maybe it was time for him to admit that the way he'd been going wasn't such a healthy way to live.

Shannon whirled into her apartment and closed the door. She leaned against it for a moment, then propelled herself away to pace excitedly around her living room.

This was impossible. She was a fool. She couldn't love Luke. She didn't even *know* him—and sometimes she didn't much like him. That wasn't the way love was supposed to be. It was supposed to be a mutual attraction, like her parents had known, like Becca and Clay had. Love was built on respect, interests, not on hostility and suspicions.

Love certainly wasn't built on physical attraction

alone, no matter how fabulous and mind-boggling it might be.

Shannon pressed her hands against her stomach. Love wasn't supposed to hurt like this.

She spun in a circle of distress, then jolted to a stop when she spied Luke's hat. Her shoulders slumped.

Luke's hat. She walked over, removed it from the hook and turned it in her hands. Foolishly, she held it to her nose, breathing in the scent of him, the clean smell of his hair, the slight hint of perspiration, the manliness of him. Slowly, she returned it to the hook before she was tempted to take it to bed with her.

After the way she'd just run from him, she doubted he would be back tonight to get it. She would have to take it to him. He rarely came into town, but she was out and around the county every day. Of course, she could ask her aunt Katrina to return it, but that would be cowardly.

She wouldn't take it back for a few days, though. Not until she had come to terms with this shattering moment of truth.

Shannon stalled for three days, telling herself she was too busy to stop by the Crescent Ranch, that she shouldn't be making extra stops on agency time, anyway. Truthfully, she wasn't that anxious to get back to the office since Wiley's major occupations lately seemed to be finding fault with her reports, locating extra work for her or glaring at her in the outer office. He hadn't said anything about seeing her out with Luke, but he didn't have to. Wiley would never discuss something face-to-face if he could make his point with cold silences. It was annoying and made for a poor working atmosphere, but Shannon knew she hadn't done anything wrong, so she wasn't going to be the one to force a discussion.

After work one afternoon, Shannon went home and changed clothes, dressing in her nicest jeans and a blue shirt that accented her eyes. She took her hair out of its braid and brushed it so it fell to her waist like a yard of loose black satin. She justified all these preparations by telling herself that she was tired of wearing work clothes as she had done most times when she saw Luke.

Carefully, she placed Luke's hat in her car and started out for the Crescent Ranch. She doubted he was worried about his hat. If he had been, he would have called or stopped by to pick it up. On the other hand, he may have thought there was a possibility she would have had another of the crazy reactions she'd had when he'd left the hat. She didn't know *how* she was going to explain that one. She couldn't very well say, "Sorry I ran off the other night. You see, I'd just realized I'm in love with you and it shook me up."

Not a good idea, she concluded as she drove slowly along the highway behind a cattle truck.

Besides, now that she thought about it, it probably wasn't love at all. No doubt it had been nothing more than the infatuation she'd felt for Luke since she had met him. After all, she'd never been in love before. How could she possibly know how it felt? After she'd made her discovery, the only emotion she'd known was sheer terror. Love couldn't be that awful. Otherwise, why would anyone ever indulge in it?

She had a reputation for being levelheaded and logical. All she had to do was apply those principles to the emotions she'd experienced the other night, and it all made perfect sense. Attraction was natural and normal. He was an attractive man. He was appealing because he was different than the other men she knew. Different than *anyone* she knew. It was only natural that she was concerned about his place in the community. It was her job, and this community was her home.

Attraction and concern for another person weren't necessarily love. Besides, as she'd already told herself, she really didn't know what love felt like.

With a nod of satisfaction—she'd worked this out with perfect logic—Shannon made the turn into Luke's driveway and drove to the house. There was a small sedan parked in front of the house. It had the distinctive yellow license plates of New Mexico. Luke's sister had arrived.

She stopped her car, stepped out and leaned in for Luke's hat. When she straightened, she saw that he was on the porch looking at her, a slight smile on his lips, his eyes warm and inviting. Apparently he didn't hold her bizarre behavior against her. Happiness surged through her, making her feel suddenly boneless. Her heart jumped into her throat.

Oh, she thought, attempting to stiffen her suddenly weak knees. *So that's what love feels like.* It defied logic, no doubt about that.

She gave him a foolish, lopsided grin and held up the hat as she approached the porch. "Same song, second verse. I should have let you come in the other night and get your hat, but I was…" She shrugged. What on earth could she say? "I don't know what I was."

He grinned. "That's okay. I should have remembered it or come back for it sooner this week."

The words really meant nothing. Neither of them could have quoted the other ten seconds later. They weren't listening to each other because they were too busy looking into each other's eyes and grinning foolishly. Luke recovered his senses first. He stepped back and opened the screen door. "Come in. You can meet my sister and my new brother-in-law."

Shannon sensed a certain amount of satisfaction in the words and knew he was pleased that the two of them had married. She walked inside to see a young man lying in Luke's recliner. He was tall and red-haired with green eyes and a sweet smile. He cradled Cody carefully against his side and tried to rise when he saw Shannon. She quickly motioned for him to stay seated.

Luke introduced her to Steve Logan, then made introductions again when his sister walked in from the kitchen. Jeanette turned out to be a tall, model-slim, Meryl Streep look-alike with eyes of a color similar to Luke's and a shy smile. She walked right up to shake Shannon's hand.

"Luke told me how you and your great-aunt helped him out in taking care of Cody." She turned and gave her new husband and baby a misty smile. "I'm so grateful. I don't know what I would have done if not for you and my big brother." She lifted Cody from his father's arms, then turned and sat on the arm of his chair. Steve put his hand on her back and rubbed it lightly.

"We were happy to do it," Shannon answered, casting a glance at Luke. He was turning away, his face oddly stiff. With a jolt, she realized that his sister's gratitude embarrassed him. Shannon found it touching, though she knew he wouldn't have liked it if she'd told him that. He motioned for Shannon to sit on the sofa, then walked over, pulled out his desk chair and turned it to face the people in his living room.

Shannon thought it was a good sign that the man who'd been so intent on spending life as a loner just weeks ago was looking quite content at having his living room crowded with people.

She asked after Steve's injuries.

"I'll be okay in a few weeks, but my rodeoing days are over. This isn't the first time I've ended up in the hospital." He gave Jeanette and Cody a smile as he shrugged. "I can't do that anymore. I've got people depending on me now."

Jeanette leaned over and rewarded him with a kiss, and Shannon, warmed by their affection and commitment to each other, turned her gaze to Luke. He was watching them with narrowed eyes as if he was trying to puzzle something out.

"Luke's letting us stay here until I get back on my feet," Steve concluded. "Then I've got to find a job to support my family."

It was on the tip of Shannon's tongue to suggest that Luke hire Steve to work for him, but the oddly distant look on his face kept her quiet. No doubt Luke wouldn't appreciate her interference.

Cody began to fuss, and Shannon stood to leave so Jeanette could tend to him. "I hope I'll see you again," she said. "If you're feeling better, Steve, maybe you'd like to go to the Tarrant Valley rodeo next weekend. The Fourth of July rodeo is a big deal in our little town.'' She paused and grimaced. ''Unless, of course, you'd rather not watch if you can't participate.''

Steve laughed and shook his head. ''Nah. I think this time I'd just be glad it's not me out there getting stomped.''

''That makes two of us,'' Jeanette agreed as she carried Cody into the bedroom.

With a wave, Shannon turned and walked outside with Luke. When they reached her car, he held the door for her, then closed it. Before she started the motor, he pushed his hands into his back pockets and rocked on his heels. He stuck his tongue in his cheek and said, ''I realize I haven't known you long, but I never took you to be an underhanded woman.''

''I'm not!''

''You're determined to get me to that rodeo, aren't you?''

She gave him an innocent look. ''Why, Luke, whatever do you mean?''

His soft breath of laughter warmed her. It sounded so much more natural than that rusty laugh she'd heard from him before. ''You're determined to get me out and have me meet the people of this community, aren't you?''

''I've never made any secret of that.''

Luke leaned over and placed his forearms on the window she'd rolled down. ''I'm not your project, Shannon.''

She looked up with an irrepressible grin. ''No, you're not, but until you're ready to participate in my project, you'll have to do. A girl's got to do something to keep busy.'' She started her car, wiggled her fingers at him and drove away, leaving him grinning after her.

Kids shrieked, barreling through the stands as they chased each other, endangering people who scattered to get out of their way while mothers called to stop them. The smell of hot dogs and coffee drifted from the refreshment booths. The public address system squealed, then settled down and the announcer began speaking. No one could understand a word he said.

Shannon sat beside her mother, munched on popcorn and reveled in the day. The Fourth of July was her favorite holiday. Most people chose Christmas or Thanksgiving, even Valentine's Day, but she'd always loved the fourth in Tarrant because it meant an early morning parade with every civic group, Scout troop and musical ensemble participating. She'd often wondered where the audience that lined Tarrant's main street came from, since everyone in town seemed to be in the parade.

Next came a family picnic, then the rodeo, where there had always been some family members participating. At the end of the day when everyone was exhausted and ready to head home, there were fireworks. She loved every minute of it.

Her family was gathered in the stands waiting to see how their friends and neighbors would perform in the various events against the few professionals who came. Becca and Clay sat nearby, Clay holding Christina and shading her with an umbrella. Shannon hid a smile at the sight of her mining engineer brother-in-law holding the delicately dressed baby girl and the pink umbrella.

Becca was applying an ice pack to Jimmy's knee. He'd fallen and scraped it when he'd joined the other kids in chasing a pig. He hadn't won, and Shannon knew her sister was secretly thrilled because the prize for winning had been the beleaguered piglet. No way would Becca welcome a pig to root around in her garden.

Brittnie was there, too, with her new husband, Jared Cruz, for once dressed not in a business suit, but in jeans and a T-shirt. Shannon almost hadn't recognized him without a tie. Nearby, Jared's grandfather, Roberto, sat holding hands with Great-aunt Katrina.

Brittnie leaned over and tapped Shannon on the shoulder. "I don't know about you, but I think that if Roberto and Aunt Kat start kissing the way they did at the family Memorial Day picnic, Jared needs to throw some ice on them."

Shannon burst out laughing. "Great idea. We can't have any more X-rated family get-togethers. It's a bad influence on the kids."

She turned to watch as the first competition was announced. Her attention was snagged by a group of people who had stopped at the bottom of the crowded stands. She was delighted to see that one of them was Luke, though she didn't see his family. Excitedly, she stood and waved to get his attention, then urged her family to scoot over and make room.

Luke joined them and Shannon happily introduced him around. Katrina jumped up and gave him a hug, which he accepted with a look of surprise. She asked after Cody. He assured her that the baby was fine, then sat beside Shannon and Mary Jane, who greeted him warmly and excused herself to sit with a friend she hadn't seen in a while.

"Steve didn't feel like coming today, after all. His head still hurts him quite a bit," Luke said.

Shannon, overcoming a ridiculous urge to sit and grin stupidly at him, managed to get her joy under control. "That's too bad," she said. "But I'm glad you could come. Have they made plans for what they'll do when he's well?"

"No, not yet."

"You could hire him to work for you," she blurted.

Luke abandoned any interest in what was happening in the arena and looked at her. "I can?"

Heat flooded her cheeks. "Sure. You need help. He needs a job."

"He might require payment, since he's got a wife and baby to take care of," Luke noted.

She blinked at him. "Well, of course."

He shook his head. "Listen, Miss Fix-it, did it ever occur to you that maybe the reason I don't hire help is because I can't afford it?"

"Uh, no." She opened and closed her mouth a couple of times, unable to think of anything to add.

"Buying the Crescent took everything I had. I'll work alone until I can afford to hire some hands. I'd like to help Steve and Jeanette. She's not going to get what she deserves from her mother unless we wrestle it away from Catherine, but running myself into debt to hire Steve, or any help, for that matter, won't help anybody." His lionlike eyes fixed on hers. "End of discussion," he said.

"Okay," she answered meekly, then sat back to

stare at the action before them. On the one hand, she was sorry Luke was financially strapped. On the other hand, she was stunned that he'd told her about it. She would love to think that meant something significant, that he was beginning to love her as she loved him. She had to be realistic, though. No doubt, she'd only annoyed the daylights out of him, forcing him to tell her as much as he had.

The awkward silence between them was filled by the surging conversation of the crowd.

Luke spoke. "Aren't they your cousins?" he asked, nodding toward two men who were busy testing their ropes and checking their horses in preparation for competition. The object was for the two riders to simultaneously rope a steer as it ran across the arena.

"Yes," she answered proudly. "They rope together, work together. They can do just about anything. They've worked on ranches all their lives, and believe it or not, they're accomplished chefs. My uncle Dave got the bright idea of turning his place into a guest ranch a few years ago, and the boys wanted to help out, so they learned..." Her words trailed off as an idea erupted, full blown, in her head.

Luke glanced at her. "Learned what?" Unseeing, her eyes turned to him. He straightened in reaction to the odd look on her face. "Shannon?"

Her mind racing, it took her a few seconds to focus on what he was asking her. "The boys learned how to cook," she finished, her voice soft, her gaze drifting to stare blankly at some clouds on the horizon. Why hadn't she thought of this before? It was the perfect solution. Her jumbled thoughts piled one possibility on top of another.

Edgy, Luke touched her arm. "Shannon? What's the matter with you?"

She didn't respond, still too involved in her thoughts to listen. She held up her hand, palm out, to indicate she'd heard him. "But then Uncle Dave abandoned his plan, never did even try the guest ranch idea." She blinked, focused and took a deep breath as her eyes met his. "Luke?"

Clearly worried, he stared at her. "Yes. Shannon, are you all right?" he asked, then glanced around. "Are you overheated? Dizzy? Have you had too much sun?" He started to signal to one of her sisters, but Shannon caught his hand.

"I'm all right." Excitedly, she gripped his fingers. Her midnight blue eyes shone. "Luke, that's what you could do. It would solve all your problems."

"What?"

"You could turn your ranch into a guest ranch." She sat back as if waiting for him to applaud.

He stared at her for a full ten seconds, and then his eyes widened in complete horror. "A guest..." He looked around furtively, obviously in hopes no one had heard her. Relief crossed his face when he saw that her family and the others around them were too involved in watching the action in the arena. "You mean a *dude ranch?*"

Her face fell at his scandalized tone. Her hands clapped onto her hips. "You don't have to say it in the same voice you'd use to say cess pit," she insisted.

"Honey, I have to tell you, that's where that idea belongs." He turned away dismissively, settled his hat on his head, crossed his arms and stared straight ahead.

She knew she'd never convince him if she got angry, so she took a deep breath and said, "Don't you see, Luke? It's the perfect solution."

"Solution to what?"

"Your money troubles."

Luke leaned closer to Shannon, his eyes dark with determination. When he spoke, his voice was low and ominous. "I don't *have* money troubles. I'm not in debt. I have assets."

"Yeah, a ranch you can't afford to stock." She scoffed, foolishly ignoring the warning in his face and voice. "What you refuse to acknowledge is that your real assets are a big house with plenty of bedrooms and bathrooms that can be used for guests, a string of horses for trail rides, trails *for* riding. Violet Beardsley has access to Randall Lake from her property. She'd probably give you an easement so your guests could go to the lake for fishing, even swimming. Of course no power boats are allowed, but you could set up day trips over to other lakes for that."

Luke stared at her as if she was growing a second head even as he watched.

Undeterred, Shannon forged ahead. "And you've got help. Steve. Jeanette. It would be perfect for them. They could have the other little cottage for their home and manage the place for you. They could work for you and keep Cody right with them." The more ideas formed in her head, the faster she talked. "You don't want them to go and take him away, do you?"

"Well, no, but I—"

"You could hire Ben and Tim to do the cooking,

organize trail rides, even help you with the real ranch work. They want to stay in this area but they haven't been able to find permanent jobs. This would be perfect for them.''

"I'm not obligated to provide jobs for—''

"There are any number of other people around who would be willing to work for you. Tarrant isn't exactly brimming with industry, you know.''

He stared at her with the fascination of a cobra mesmerized by a snake charmer. When it appeared that she had finally wound down, he shook his head like a man coming out of shock. "No. Shannon, I'm a rancher. A cattleman, not a *dude ranch* owner.''

"Oh, now, Luke, quit saying it like that.''

He gave her a disgruntled look. "I can't help it. The horror of the idea just seems to spill over into my tone of voice.''

She rolled her eyes. "Luke, you know perfectly well that the cattle and livestock business can knock the stuffing out of you financially. Turning your place into a guest ranch would give you a steady income of hard cash—''

"Forget it.'' He turned sharply away and concentrated on the arena.

"At least consider it,'' she urged.

"No.''

She clenched her fists in her lap. "Ooh, you are so stubborn.''

"Yeah, we both already know that.''

She fell silent, trying to think of more arguments.

He cut a glance at her. "Quit sulking.''

"I'm not,'' she said, barely rescuing her bottom lip from sticking out and quivering.

He gave a gusty sigh. "Come on, Shannon. Can you really see me as a hotelier?"

"I admit I can't picture you standing around greeting your guests." She lifted her chin. "After all, who wants to be glared at by their host?"

"I don't glare."

"You've got a glare that could strip paint off walls."

He frowned, and the glare in question came over his face. "Forget what I said awhile back about you knowing how to be diplomatic," he advised.

"You think I've regressed?"

"To the age of dinosaurs."

Insulted, she turned away. Couldn't he see she was trying to help? Maybe she was having a hard time picturing him greeting his guests and playing the perfect host, but she knew there was a true appeal in a place like Crescent Ranch. Guest ranches were enjoying an upsurge in popularity, and there was always a special appeal about Colorado even when it wasn't ski season.

"Here's something else to consider."

"Oh, joy. She's not through yet."

She ignored his sarcasm. "I know you don't want to be part of my range management project, but I could consult with you, help you get your range back into shape. I wouldn't charge you a fee."

"How is this tied into me turning my place into a *dude ranch*?"

She shrugged. "Extra incentive?"

"Bribery."

"Won't you even consider it?"

"Absolutely not."

She laid her hand on his arm and looked at him with a melting expression in her eyes. Why couldn't he see what a great idea this was? Her voice dropped as she pleaded with him. "Please, Luke."

He tightened his arms over his chest and scowled at her. "I'll turn my place into a *dude ranch* when hell freezes over. Why can't you accept the fact that I don't want your interference? Want to work on my own. Be on my own."

"And hold your grudge as closely and tightly as possible," she retorted, hurt by his attitude. "Has it ever occurred to you that maybe you're not really mad at your stepmother, but at your father for making that unfair will?"

"You don't know what you're talking about," Luke answered in a tight, gritty voice, his eyes as sharp as lances.

She leaned close to him, pain and disillusionment brimming in her eyes. "Tell me, then, if you're so set on being a loner, why did you take Cody in, and Steve and Jeanette? Why did you come to the cattlemen's meeting, to my apartment? What are you doing here?" Unexpectedly, a tear spilled over and ran down her cheek. Her voice broke. "Why…why did you kiss me as if you couldn't get enough of me?"

Luke had no answer. He turned away. The hard set of his jaw told her he'd heard enough, that she had gone too far, said too much. She felt sick, but she couldn't take back what she'd said. Besides, what she had told him was true, though she knew she was responsible for the death of her own hopes.

CHAPTER NINE

"DID Luke leave?" Mary Jane asked Shannon, climbing off the stand to join her distraught daughter. "I was going to invite him to our family picnic over at Becca's house, then to the fireworks at the park."

Shannon watched Luke's truck disappear from the parking lot and turned blindly to her mother, distress lining her face. "He said he had to go. His sister's alone with her injured husband and the baby, and..." Her voice trailed off. She'd made up the excuse on the spur of the moment and it sounded frail even to her own ears.

She felt a sad, overwhelming disappointment in him and in herself because she'd fallen in love with him even though she'd known it could lead nowhere, and because she couldn't seem to stop trying to figure him out, change him.

"Oh, I see," Mary Jane answered tactfully, though her worried gaze studied her daughter's face. "Well, maybe we'll see him some other time."

"Sure," Shannon agreed, blinking back the tears that had spurted into her eyes. "Sure, we'll see him ag-again." Her voice broke on the last word, and she shut her mouth. There was no point in trying to fool someone who knew her so well.

Mary Jane put her arm around Shannon's waist, and Shannon placed hers around her mother's shoulders, leaning on her for support. Shannon blessed her mother's thoughtfulness in not asking questions.

Unfortunately, Brittnie and Becca weren't so tactful. They arrived a few seconds later with their families in tow.

"What's going on?" Brittnie asked, craning her neck to see where Luke had gone. "I thought he was going to stay."

"What happened?" Becca wanted to know. She hitched Christina's diaper bag onto her shoulder. "It looked like you two were arguing. I didn't know you were far enough along in your relationship for arguments."

Shannon pinched her lips together and gave her sisters a look. "We don't even *have* a relationship, so how could we argue about it?" She wasn't about to tell them her true feelings, but behind Becca and Brittnie, she saw Jared give Clay a shall-we-have-a-talk-with-this-guy kind of look. Clay answered with a tiny shake of his head.

Before anyone could ask any more questions, Jimmy scooted beside her and tucked his hand into hers. "You mad, Shannon?"

She blinked at him. "No, of course not."

"You're sad, though, huh?"

She wanted to drop the whole subject, but she certainly couldn't lie to him. "A little," she admitted.

Jimmy released a mighty sigh. "Well, if that guy won't be your boyfriend, I could be, except..." He rolled his bright eyes at her, paused and followed up with an apologetic look. "I've got me a girl, and she's the jealous type."

The family burst out laughing.

"The jealous type? Did you teach him that?" Becca asked Clay, staring at her son in bemusement.

"No," Clay declared, but he was laughing so hard, no one believed him.

Shannon knelt beside Jimmy and gave him a hug. "Thanks for the thought, sport. I really appreciate it, but I guess I'd better get my own boyfriend."

"Okay." He shrugged, then looked around at his family with a puzzled smile as if he couldn't figure out why they were chuckling at him.

In unspoken agreement, they changed the topic, making plans for the evening and speculating on whether the clouds that were massing to the south would hold off with their load of rain until after the fireworks display.

The support of her family cheered her, but Shannon felt Luke's loss out of all proportion to its importance—or what she knew should be its importance to her. She was being foolish. He hadn't invited her to love him, and he wouldn't welcome it if he knew.

An unusually wet weather system stalled over southern Colorado, and the skies alternately poured, drizzled and dripped for a week after the Fourth of July celebrations. That was fine with Shannon. It suited her mood perfectly. Whenever she thought about the suggestion she'd made to Luke and his cavalier dismissal of it, her heart ached. Whenever she thought of what she'd said about the grudge he was holding, she cringed.

She'd been overly enthusiastic about the guest ranch idea and too blunt in her assessment of him, she decided as she started out one morning to check reports of flooding around Dove Creek.

"And it's time to move on," she muttered to herself, pulling off the highway onto a back road that ran behind the Beardsley ranch. "You've been obsessing about it—about him—for a week, and nothing's improved."

She hadn't seen Luke since he'd left her at the rodeo and headed home, seemingly eager to get away from her. She would probably see him today. There was no choice. Dove Creek ran across his land, too. She already suspected that the flooding Violet had reported was caused by the water rushing across Luke's land, too effluent to stay in its channel and unable to soak into the damaged earth.

Now that the rain had stopped, she knew she could check the creek and document the full extent of the damage. Easing the truck over the rutted road took some maneuvering, but she finally managed to reach the creek. She walked along the gouged bank and saw that the damage was as bad as she'd been led to expect. Water churned and tumbled below her, taking Violet's valuable topsoil with it. Soil she and Shannon had worked hard to maintain.

Shannon looked across the distant fence toward Luke's land and knew it was even worse over there. Though she wasn't sure what good it would do, she knew she would have to go talk to him, ask his permission to check for damage on his land so she would know what to expect when yet another rainstorm came.

With a deep breath, she returned to the truck, then made her way off Violet's land and onto Luke's.

When she approached his small cottage, she saw that there were no lights on against the gloom of the gray afternoon. But the second cottage glowed with brightness, and Jeanette's car was parked out front. Shannon stopped there.

Jeanette answered the door, holding Cody against one shoulder and with a dish towel draped over the other one. The scent of baking cookies swept out to greet Shannon, making her mouth water. Jeanette invited her inside and pressed a handful of cookies on her.

"We've moved in here while Steve recovers so we won't be crowding Luke," she said, looking around the place she was making into a temporary home. "Since we're not in the same house anymore, he doesn't always tell me where he's going. Maybe Steve knows. He's out in the barn, mending tack."

Shannon thanked her for the cookies and started for the barn, thinking that Jeanette was making a cozy nest for her little family. It was too bad she would have to give it up when her husband was well. Shannon took an appreciative bite of cookie, which was a concoction of chocolate, nuts and coconut. The woman had real potential as a baker.

She found Steve in the barn, seated gingerly on a bale of hay with a couple of bridles and several tools spread out before him. He stopped work to tell her that Luke had ridden off a little while before, but he didn't know when he would be back. "I don't think he'd care if you looked at the creek," Steve said. "After all, he's the one who would benefit from your help."

Smiling ruefully, Shannon returned to the agency

truck. If Steve could figure that out, why was Luke so resistant to the idea?

She made her way to Dove Creek and found what she had expected. Water had scoured the creek's channel, then tumbled rocks, tree limbs, sagebrush and other detritus into a huge pile that stopped up the creek and sent water flooding over the land where it sloughed off, taking away what little healthy vegetation there was.

The sight depressed and saddened her. It could have been prevented, could still be stopped from happening again. Working by himself, it would take Luke days to clear it. With help, it could be done in a few hours, but he wouldn't accept help.

Her mind on Luke rather than on where she was going, Shannon stepped close to the edge of the bank. Looking down, she discovered the bank had been badly undercut by the rampaging water. She started to back up, but it was too late. Her boot heels dug into the soft earth. It crumbled and the ground gave beneath her.

"Oh!" Her arms flew up as her feet skidded out from under her.

One second she was on the bank, the next, she was skidding and scrambling down to the creek, one leg banging into a boulder, the other stretched out, scoring a gouge in the mud.

The breath was knocked out of her. Rocks and twigs tore at her clothing. A sharp stick speared her shirtsleeve, leaving a deep scrape on her arm. She barely noticed the pain because she was trying to keep her footing and stay out of the creek.

She hit it anyway, landing with her left leg twisted

beneath her. She turned, trying to keep from going in headfirst. The water pulled at her, jerking her legs down, sucking her in waist deep, filling her boots so they weighed her down as she tried to grasp for rocks or roots, anything that would keep her above water. Hidden rocks and limbs pummeled her, but she couldn't seem to avoid them.

"Shannon!"

She heard a shout and looked to see Luke's anxious face. He was lying full length at the edge of the slide looking down at her. Gratitude and hope sprang up when she saw that he had a rope in his hand. Hurriedly, he made a loop in it, ready to throw it to her.

"Can you tie this around your waist?" he shouted.

"Sure, I... Oh." She had reached up with her injured arm, and pain shot through her. "I... I don't know. My arm." She indicated her torn shirt and the blood that was seeping through. Water swept up, drenching her to the neck. She gritted her teeth against the pain of sand and dirt scraping over the torn flesh.

"I'll be right there."

She knew he didn't expect an answer, so she concentrated on keeping her grip on a tangle of roots, staying close to the edge of the creek, away from the heavy rush of water that sucked at her. Tilting her head, she watched for him to return.

While she clung there, Luke disappeared, then came back. She knew he had tied the rope to something, probably the truck bumper. He took a grip on the rope, and moving backward like a mountain climber, he inched down to her.

At one point, he looked over his shoulder to reassure her. "Hold on, honey. I'm coming."

Shannon's heart bounced into her throat when she heard the endearment, then again with dread when she saw his feet give way, but he only dangled for a second before he found his footing once again and resumed the descent.

"Here," he said, planting his boots firmly against the side of the bank. It didn't look any more stable than it had a few minutes ago, but somehow her fear had subsided. He reached down, clasped her around the waist and lifted her out of the water. "Grab the rope," he commanded.

Shaken, she obeyed. He held on with one hand and swung out of the way so she could go ahead of him, then he was back, his arms around her, his hands supporting hers on the rope, his body behind her, between her and the raging water.

"Come on, honey," he said. "You can do it." With gentle pressure, he urged her upward, and she found the strength to climb hand over hand up the slope, although her arm hurt every time she lifted it. Luke's reassuring presence was behind her every step. Finally, she reached the top.

Crawling on her hands and knees, she crept across the earth, putting as much distance as possible between herself and the creek. She stayed that way, her head down as she gulped in air. The entire episode had lasted less than ten minutes, but it seemed much longer. She had a crazy urge to kiss the damp but solid ground beneath her.

Luke was beside her in seconds, pushing her hair out of her face and turning her to look at him.

"Are you all right?"

Shannon focused on him and saw that he was bare-headed. Her hand came up shakily. "Your hat," she said faintly. "You lost it."

He gave her a wild look. "What the hell does that matter? You almost lost your *life*."

"But I didn't. You saved me."

He saw the shock in her eyes. He clenched his jaw and drew his mouth down in a harsh line. "Yeah, well, that was the damnedest stroke of luck. I just happened to see the truck, then you standing on the bank. Then you disappeared."

"But you came and saved me," she said again, still unable to believe it. "You saved my life."

He put his arms around her, found that she was shivering. "Shannon, you're in shock. Let's get you to the truck."

As soon as he said it, thunder clapped. They looked up, neither having noticed that the sky had darkened. Another wave of the storm was threatening them. Lightning was popping and flashing in the distance and moving in their direction.

Luke breathed a curse. "Just what we need." He got to his feet, then pulled her up. She sagged against him, and her shivers deepened to shudders. Lingering fright and reaction combined with cold that started deep inside and shimmered outward in waves.

"I'm sorry," she said helplessly. She tried to stand on her own, but her legs wouldn't hold her.

With an angry growl, Luke swept her into his arms. She started to protest, but he said, "Be still or I'll drop you."

She froze, then gave up the fight and allowed her

head to find its natural resting place on his shoulder. Within a few strides, he had reached the truck. Carefully, he deposited her inside, then rushed to Dusty. He removed the gelding's saddle and bridle, gave him a slap on the rump and shouted for him to go home. The horse took off at a loping pace, heading for the barn. Luke tossed the gear into the back of the truck, jerked a tarp over it, then climbed in beside Shannon and started the motor just as the heavens opened up and rain poured down in sheets. He turned slowly and headed across the fields.

"I can't see to drive in this," he shouted over the din of the rain hitting the metal roof. "We'll go to the cabin and get warmed up."

Shannon was shivering so badly that when she tried to nod, her head bobbed uncontrollably. Luke flipped on the heater, sending a rush of warmth through the cab.

"Will Dusty be okay?" she asked, her teeth chattering.

"Yeah. If he can outrun the lightning."

She gasped in horror.

Luke shook his head. "Don't worry. He'll be home before we get to the cabin. He's got a compass built into his nose. That horse can always find a feed bag."

"Won't Jeanette worry?"

"If they notice I'm not home, they'll figure I know what I'm doing." He gave her a glance, and she saw his hands tighten on the steering wheel. "Unlike you. What the hell were you doing standing on that bank?" he asked with a sudden burst of fury.

"How was I supposed to know it would give way?" she asked, tears starting. She was horrified because she rarely cried, but she didn't seem to have any control over her reactions. She felt strangely disjointed, as if everything was either in fast forward or slow motion.

"You're supposed to be an expert on water control," he yelled. "Couldn't you see that the water in that creek was *out* of control?"

Sudden fury shot through her, steadying her and sending heat rushing to warm her. "And whose fault is that? Who is it that won't let me start a project that could get that water under control?"

His head snapped around to hers. "You think your foolishness was *my* fault?"

"It wasn't foolishness. I was doing my job."

"What the hell kind of job would you have been doing if you'd gotten yourself killed?"

They reached the cabin. She was saved from answering, which was good because she had no answer. She wasn't about to tell him she hadn't been watching what she was doing because she'd been busy thinking about him. He stopped the truck and prepared to climb out. "Is there a first aid kit in this thing?" he asked.

"In the glove compartment," she answered. Though she was still angry with him, she wasn't crazy and she did need to doctor her arm.

He grabbed the kit, then pulled her toward him and got them both out of the truck.

Any part of them that wasn't already muddy or wet was instantly drenched as they made the dash through the pouring rain to the cabin. Luke whirled her inside and slammed the door, then hurried around closing the shutters over the windows. The barest specks of afternoon light filtered through the shutters, bringing the room to almost total darkness.

"I'll start a fire," he said. "Better get out of those wet things."

The few seconds of warmth she had known in the truck had fled. Once again shudders were racking her. She stood stupidly, unable to coordinate her numb fingers to unbutton her shirt. Who could have guessed she could be so cold in July?

From somewhere, Luke miraculously conjured kindling, logs and a match. He had the fire started within moments. The flame blazed up, illuminating the room. Immediately, he turned and saw that she stood where he had left her with her fingers plucking helplessly at her blouse.

"I can't," she said, lifting tear-filled eyes to him and letting her nerveless hands fall to her sides. Her anger had fled, leaving her curiously drained, as if she was waiting for some new emotion to fill her up. She didn't want that emotion to be self-pity, so she blinked back the tears.

Instantly, Luke was before her. "Let me," he said, his voice low and gruff, reaching for her buttons. "I've got to doctor that cut on your arm."

She tried to bat his hands away. "Not if you're going to be mad at me."

He ignored her efforts to evade him. "I'm not mad."

"Promise?"

"I promise." He led her to the same cot where he'd carried her the day they met and eased her down as carefully as he had that time.

"Then why did you yell at me?" she asked sadly.

"Because I was scared, Shannon." His voice was low and steady. His eyes met hers. "More scared than I've ever been before in my life." He knelt in front of her and worked her wet boots off her feet, then peeled off her socks.

"You shouldn't yell at people when you're scared," she informed him, then ruined her righteous tone by sniffing tearfully.

"Then you'd better quit scaring me," he suggested, pulling her to her feet and propping her up like a rag doll so he could unfasten her jeans and slide down the zipper.

Though she was still in shock, some part of Shannon's brain told her she should protest the fact that he was maneuvering her wet jeans over her hips, rolling them down her legs and tossing them on a chair. After all, she wondered hazily, why should he have to strip her in order to doctor her arm?

It all seemed perfectly natural, though. Shannon, who was strong, reliable, independent, who wanted to be known for her brains and abilities rather than her beauty, didn't seem to mind at all that Luke Farraday was unbuttoning her blouse. She lifted her head to focus on his face, only inches from hers.

"You shouted at me, and now you're frowning at me."

"I'm concentrating," he grunted. She noticed that his hands weren't quite steady.

"Humph," she answered. "You're undressing me."

"So?" His voice seemed to be coming from his toes, his fingers lingering over each button as if they had turned clumsy and he could barely work the buttons through the holes.

"So I'd think you could look like you're enjoying it a little bit."

His hands jerked. A button popped off and flew across the room.

"Oh!" She watched it with strange distraction. Was this the aftermath of an adrenaline rush? She seemed to be disconnected from her body, and yet she felt her mind, her thoughts, reaching out to wrap around Luke.

His eyes came up to meet hers. "What did you say?" he choked the words out.

"You could act like you're enjoying undressing me. After all, my boots are off, my pants are off, my blouse is almost off." She looked down and frowned. "Do you think you're going to take off my bra and panties? They're wet, too."

Another button flew across the room, landing on the wooden floor with a soft clatter.

"Luke, why are you popping off my buttons? They're flying around like popcorn." She gave him a serious look. "You know, I won't be able to button my blouse ever again if you don't stop doing that."

"Give me strength," he groaned.

"Strength for what?"

Luke cursed under his breath and finally managed to free her last few buttons and pull her wet shirt off her arms. He ignored her question and asked one of his own. He flipped open the first aid kit and removed the items he needed as he asked, "Shannon, have you been drinking?"

"Maybe I swallowed some creek water," she answered dutifully. He sat beside her on the cot and swabbed at the cut with some antiseptic, then slapped a bandage on it none too gently. When he started to stand up, Shannon placed a hand on his arm, holding him beside her. She leaned closer to him, her blue eyes deeply worried. "Does my breath smell like mud? Because I don't want it to smell like mud."

With the expression of a man being tortured on a rack, Luke met her eyes. "Oh, Shannon, you're killing me."

Shannon lifted her arms and placed them around his shoulders. "Oh, I'm sorry, Luke." Her voice trembled with sympathy as she tilted her head back and looked into his eyes. "I didn't mean to do that. Here, I'll kiss it better."

"Oh, God," he groaned.

When her lips touched his, lightning exploded between them, more powerful than anything that was happening outside. His lips were hard in demand, then soft in giving, opening over hers with fire and lust raging. Shannon threaded her hands into his hair, tilting her head to give herself greater access to him. This was what she had wanted, she thought, wild with elation. She had wanted him to kiss her, to make her feel the same love and warmth she felt for him.

He pulled his mouth away, rolling his forehead against hers as if he couldn't quite bear to break the contact. "Shannon, we've got to stop this. This is getting way out of hand, and you're in no shape for—" He broke off.

"What kind of shape do I have to be in, Luke?" she asked. She couldn't have said where her boldness was coming from, except that her fright in the creek had somehow short-circuited her instinct for self-preservation as well as the common sense she was so proud of. Her bottom lip stuck out. "Don't you like my shape?"

"Oh, murder," he groaned. "Shannon, don't sulk."

"Why do you always say that to me? I don't sulk."

"I say it because whenever you sulk, it makes me want to do this." His mouth touched hers again, and she felt him drawing her bottom lip between his lips, gently sucking it in an erotic way that sent heat flashing through her.

"Ooh, Luke," she breathed. "I feel like I'm going to explode."

"Me, too," he admitted, his mouth making a trail from her lips to her jaw, then to her collarbone. He put his arms around her, but his fingers tangled in her loose braid, still damp from her dunking. "Here," he said. "Let me fix this."

For an instant, she thought he was going to fasten the tie holding her braid, but instead, she felt his fingers, swift and sure, unbraiding her hair, spreading it over her shoulders, smoothing the damp locks down her back.

"Now," he said, his voice rich with appreciation, "I can do what I've been wanting to." He dove his hands into her hair, fisting it gently and drawing her head back so that his lips could ravage her mouth.

Though she was shaking with excitement and arousal, she managed to duck away from him. She put a hand in the middle of his chest, feeling the damp material of his shirt, surprised that it didn't begin steaming from the heat they were generating.

Firelight played over them. Luke's gaze, smoldering and focused on her, sent thrills through her. "What are you asking?" he said in a raspy voice.

She swallowed, suddenly nervous, unsure but determined to go ahead. "Make love to me, Luke. Please?"

His eyes widened. "Shannon, this isn't…"

"Isn't what you had in mind? It's what I've got in mind." She lifted her chin. In for a penny, in for a pound. "It's what I've had in mind for a long time."

He opened his mouth, shook his head, seemingly unable to form an answer.

"Do I scare you?"

"Hell, yes!"

"Good, because you've been scaring me since the moment we met." She didn't expand on that because she wasn't sure she could explain without admitting she loved him, and that was a secret she wanted to keep for a little while longer. She took a deep breath. "Are you going to make me beg you, Luke?"

"No," he said, though his voice seemed to close on the word. "I'm not that much of a fool."

He laid her gently on the cot. It was covered with a clean blanket. She ran her hand over it.

"I stocked this place in case I ever needed it. Looks like I do."

"Yes." Forgetting the blanket, she held up her arms. "And I need you, Luke."

He didn't require a second invitation. Luke stood and removed his clothes swiftly. Shannon's mouth went dry at his physical perfection. "The first time I ever saw you, I thought you had a great backside," she told him. "It's even better than I imagined."

His face went stiff, and she knew she'd embarrassed him. She laughed softly at his expression. "I'm sure you've been told that before."

He came down beside her and took her in his arms. "Not by someone I—" He kissed her, cutting off his own words.

Shannon meant to ask what he'd started to say, but his hands were on her, running over her skin with need, warmth, urgency.

Excitement began to build between them, heightened by whispered words of desire. Shannon touched him in all the places she had fantasized about, running her hands over his hard muscles, down his arms, over his chest, then lower to touch his manhood. His breath sizzled in her ear.

"Shannon," he said. "Shannon, you don't know what you do to me."

"I know what you do to me," she whispered. "You make me feel like the most desirable woman on earth."

"You are." He laughed. "Believe me, you are."

He turned her then, settling over her, drawing her close, readying her to accept him. Her back arched as he came to her, teeth gritted against a moment of pain.

He stopped, shocked, staring into her eyes. "Shannon, I…"

She reached to hold him when she thought he might pull away. "Luke, this is for you," she whispered, then he began to move, and the fulfillment he created was for both of them.

CHAPTER TEN

"WHY didn't you tell me?"

Shannon's hand stopped. She had been smoothing it over the soft hair on Luke's chest—the only soft thing about him. After he made love to her, he covered them with the blanket and gathered her in his arms. Between the dying fire, the blanket and the heat his body generated, it was going to be a hot arrangement once the storm cleared. She didn't mind. She was so giddily in love with him she wouldn't have minded if he'd been holding her in a steaming sauna.

When he spoke, she could feel the vibration against her ear. "Shannon, why didn't you tell me?" he repeated.

She lifted her head and met his gaze. "Tell you what, Luke?"

His eyes had gone dark and troubled. "That you had never been with a man before. Didn't you think I had a right to know?"

Shannon didn't like the coolness in his voice. It chilled her in places that had been warm only moments before. He still held her in his arms, yet she felt as if he'd stepped back ten feet. "I didn't really think about it at all. And, besides, when would I have told you? When we first met? A week ago?"

"An hour ago would have been fine," he answered in a dry tone.

"Come on, Luke. Neither of us were thinking very clearly."

He gazed at her for long moments, then said, "You're right. There's something else we didn't think about. Birth control. Shannon, I swear to you, I've never taken a chance like that before. Is there any chance you could have gotten pregnant?"

An automatic denial shot to her lips, but she did a quick mental calculation of her cycle, and her eyes flew to his. He didn't need to hear her admit it. She cleared her throat. "Um, I guess we'll know in a few weeks, won't we?"

"I'm not willing to wait a few weeks."

She didn't like the sound of that. "What do you mean?"

Luke sat up, drawing her with him. His voice calm and steady, he put his hands on her shoulders and forced her to look at him as he said, "We'll be married immediately."

Stunned, she stared. "What?"

He wrapped the blanket around her, sat up and gathered his clothes. He shook out his damp, mud-stiffened jeans and pulled them on. "I said we'll be married right away."

"No," she stammered. "That isn't necessary. We don't even know if—"

"Yes." He leaned over her, his eyes glittering in the dimly lit room. His voice was implacable. "It is necessary. If you're pregnant, it's my baby, and it's not going to be born with any whispers about its legitimacy."

"Oh, Luke, people don't really worry about that anymore—"

"I do!" He shoved a thumb toward his chest, then turned and grabbed his shirt. He shook it out and stuffed his arms into it.

"You're overreacting," Shannon pointed out.

"I'm taking care of my responsibilities," he answered in a grim tone.

"You don't *have* any responsibilities here." Growing angry at his stubborn insistence, she jabbed a thumb at her chest. "I'm responsible for my own actions. Do you think I waited until I was twenty-seven to make love with a man because I'm irresponsible? Because I don't know what I'm doing?"

Luke's hand shot out in swift dismissal. "You said yourself that neither of us were thinking very clearly."

"I'm certainly thinking *now,*" she said, tightening the blanket around herself and throwing her head back as she glared at him. Her black hair swept across her shoulders as she shook her head. "I'm thinking that you're resorting to your usual high-handed stubbornness."

"Get used to it," he answered furiously. He ran his hands through his hair.

"*What?*" She couldn't believe he was being so unreasonable.

"Shannon, I'm not going to make the same mistake my father did."

"What mistake? What are you talking about?"

"My stepmother tricked him into marriage. After my mother died, he went kind of crazy for a while. Drank much of the time, neglected the ranch, the house, land, everything. Met Catherine in a bar one night. He was fair game for someone like her who was looking for an easy ride.''

"What's that got to do with—"

"She deliberately got pregnant with Jeanette because she knew he would marry her. She told me that years later,'' he added, his eyes furious.

Shannon surged to her knees, clasped the blanket around herself and stared at him in outrage. "Are you suggesting that I would try to trick—"

"No, of course not. But we're not going to take any chances. We're going to do things in the right order." He grabbed his socks and put them on, then stomped his feet into his boots. "My dad neglected his responsibilities, let things drift until he got himself into a mess. I'm not going to do that."

In spite of her annoyance with him, Shannon felt a flash of sympathy as she recalled the messy will his father had left. She had to make him understand how she felt, though. "Luke, I make my own decisions."

"This wasn't a decision," he said, gesturing toward the bunk. "It was lust, need, a reaction to danger. Something I swore I'd never do, but it's done now, and we'll deal with it."

Hurt stabbed through her. How could he cheapen it like that? "No," she whispered, but he didn't hear her.

He was busy buttoning his shirt, rolling up the sleeves, avoiding looking at her. "And do you want to be known as the scientist who couldn't figure out how to keep from getting pregnant?"

His arguments were coming from so many directions at once, she couldn't follow them. "That's ridiculous. I keep telling you I'm responsible for my-self.''

''Well, you're not alone in this. Besides, do you want to risk embarrassing your family?''

He had her there, and they both knew it. They stared at each other across the darkened room. Backlit by the dying fire, he stood with his hands on his hips, his wide shoulders set stiffly.

She wanted to read his expression, to see some softness, some hint of his feelings for her, but she saw nothing but his usual calm, direct gaze.

He broke away first. ''The rain's stopped. You'd better get dressed,'' he said, picking up his boots and turning toward the door. ''Do you need help?'' he asked, indicating her bandaged arm.

''No. I don't need anything from you.'' Her harsh tone made him pause, but she wouldn't meet his eyes. He walked out and left her alone, closing the door behind him.

Shannon wanted to throw something, preferably at him. No, she thought furiously as she scooted off the bed and gathered her damp, dirty clothes. They were clammy and uncomfortable on her skin.

She didn't need anything from him except maybe a few words of love, an indication that he cared about her. His only concern was avoiding embarrassment. What kind of proposal was that? What kind of marriage could they possibly have, with that as its basis?

None, obviously. She wasn't going to be forced into marriage on the very slight possibility that she might be pregnant. As furious as she was with Luke right now, she understood what was motivating him to insist on marriage. She still wasn't going to do it, though, no matter how much she loved him, because, very simply, he didn't love her. He saw marriage to her as his duty. There had to be more than that to a marriage.

Shaking with reaction, disappointment and lingering anger, Shannon managed to get her jeans and shirt on, but her socks and boots were too damp. She couldn't even slide her feet into them. She decided to drive barefoot. It was dangerous, because her feet were wet, but she had no choice. She wanted to get in the truck and start driving as fast and as far away as possible. Then she wouldn't have to marry a man who didn't love her.

With crazy, disjointed thoughts flying around in her head, Shannon left the cabin. When she climbed behind the steering wheel of the truck, Luke went in to douse the fire. He came back almost immediately and climbed in beside her.

They made their slow way across the range, following a muddy path made worse by the downpour. Neither of them said a word. Shannon's scraped arm ached, but she gritted her teeth and kept driving. In fact, she ached in places she'd never ached before, and memories of what had happened brought a confusing rush of awe, tenderness and anger at Luke. And at herself.

As they neared the ranch buildings, Luke finally spoke. "You'd better go straight home and take care of that arm. Have you had a tetanus shot recently?"

She shot him a furious look. Her whole life had changed, and he was asking her about a tetanus shot? "Yes," she snapped. "Right after the first time you kissed me."

His head whipped around, but he didn't ask why she was angry. The darkness in his eyes lightened with a hint of respect, as if he was pleased with her. "I'll come over this evening," he said when she stopped in front of his cottage. "And we'll make plans."

"You can come over, but we won't be making any plans. We have a few things to get straight." She pulled away before he could answer, before he was out of the truck. He gave her a surprised look as he scrambled to get out and close the door. Good, she thought as she pressed on the gas pedal. Maybe he'd quit thinking he was going to have things all his own way.

As she turned in the driveway, Shannon saw Jeanette rush to the porch of her cottage and call to her brother. Luke approached her, his hands out placatingly as if to reassure her.

Shannon wondered why he couldn't be bothered to placate her. Offer a few words of love or comfort. Anything rather than the cold, calm way he'd announced that they would be getting married, and the reasons.

She had news for him. She made her own decisions and she was going to tell him exactly that—again—when he showed up at her apartment.

Shannon paced her living room. She had showered, washed her hair, dried it, curled it, then told herself she was being an idiot and brushed it out so that it fell in a shiny wave to her waist. She'd put on her favorite turquoise sweater and skirt, though she thought there was a possibility that black might be a more appropriate color for this strange engagement of hers.

She had thought about calling her sisters or her mother, but this wasn't something she could share yet.

Sitting on her sofa, she put her face in her hands and tried to think of a way out of this. She hadn't come up with a single workable idea when she heard Luke's knock on the door. Her heart skittered around in her chest as if looking for a place to hide.

Striving for calmness, she stood, smoothed her skirt and walked to the door. She manufactured a cool expression, which collapsed into astonishment when she saw not Luke but Wiley Frost standing on the threshold.

"Wiley, what are you doing here?" She was so stunned, she didn't even resist when he pushed past her and stalked into her apartment.

As he swept by, she saw that he was dressed in new slacks and a neatly pressed shirt. His hair was combed, and he was wearing enough cologne to anesthetize a mule. "I want to know where you were this afternoon. You weren't back at the office by the time I left. Did you do something to the truck?"

Her mouth open, she stared at him. "Wiley, are you kidding? I don't have to answer to you for every one of my working hours. I was doing my job, and as usual, I took the truck to do it."

He turned to her, his colorless eyes narrowing to slits. "You were with Luke Farraday, weren't you?"

Her start of surprise was all he needed to see. He stepped up to her, and she realized that she had far underestimated how much he disliked her.

"What's he got, anyway?" Wiley asked, sneering.

"He's not rich. All he's got is that ranch. Sunk all his money into it."

"That's none of your business," she spluttered. What on earth was the matter with him? Where was this crazy behavior coming from?

"Are you screwing him?"

She gasped in outrage, but she didn't have to reply. In a blur of movement, Luke came in the open door and grabbed Wiley by the front of his shirt. Wiley squawked in surprise as Luke backed him up against the wall and lifted him so that his feet barely touched the floor.

"What did you say to my fiancée?" Luke asked, his lips barely moving.

"Your...your fiancée?" Wiley wheezed, his eyes rolling. "Since when?"

"That's not your concern. Just remember that she's going to marry me. I'm going to be taking care of certain things for her from now on, and one of those things is you."

"You don't know what you're doing," Wiley retorted. "She's not what you think she is. She leads men on. She led me on, said she wanted me, and then—aah!"

Luke tightened his grip on Wiley's shirt and slid one hand up to jerk his tie around his neck. Wiley's eyes bugged from their sockets.

"You've got that wrong, don't you, Wiley? She didn't want you, and no matter how much you wanted her, she wouldn't have you. She wants me, Wiley, and that's eating your guts out, isn't it?"

Wiley's face was turning purple, but Luke didn't slacken his grip. "You don't know what you're doing," her boss insisted. "You think you know her, but you don't. She's got papers all filled out to get government types on your land, telling you what to do, what to grow, where to graze. I've seen the papers. They're in her desk."

Luke's eyes shot to her face. Puzzled, she shrugged, then she remembered the papers she'd begun filling out when she had thought Ben and Timmy would be buying the Crescent. Her eyes widened in alarm.

His face went stiff as if he was assessing this revelation and her reaction to it. Then he pulled Wiley away from the wall and began marching him toward the door.

"For your information, you little twerp, she was doing her job. But that won't be any of your business from now on, Wiley, because you're not going to be working in that office anymore."

"What are you talking about? I'm the boss. I'm—"

"You're going to quit, Wiley, and you're going to find a new job, or Shannon is going to file sexual harassment charges against you. If she's too nice to do that, I might just decide it would be pleasant exercise to beat the hell out of you." He frog-marched Wiley into the hall and shoved him away. "If you're smart, and I don't think you are, you'll write out your resignation tonight and get out of Tarrant by morning. If I see you again, I might not be so nice."

Wiley began to protest, but when Luke started for him again, he turned and staggered down the hall, his hands gripping his bruised throat.

Luke watched him go, then turned and stepped inside her apartment. He closed the door, then pointed a finger at her. "Explain about the papers," he commanded.

Shannon straightened, her blue eyes stormy. "Luke, you don't think I would have—"

"I don't know what to think," he said in a controlled voice. "Because *you* haven't explained yet."

She stared at him while thoughts flew through her mind. This was going to be a fine marriage if he was willing to take Wiley's word over hers. But he wasn't, she reminded herself, and given his history with his family, he probably felt he needed an explanation. She took a breath to control the angry pounding of her heart. "They were grant application forms. I started filling them out when I thought Ben and Tim were going to be able to buy the Crescent. Since they were already partly done, I kept them in my desk in case you ever wanted to apply for the money."

He shook his head in mystified fury. "I told you the first time we met that I didn't want government money or interference."

She threw her hands in the air. "I thought you might change your mind. How was I supposed to know you'd stay as stubborn as you were on that day? For all I knew, you might have turned out to be a perfectly reasonable man. Of course, I *know* better now!"

Luke stared at her for several seconds, then his lips twitched. "Yeah, I guess you do." He breathed a hearty sigh. "I'm sorry. I know you wouldn't do anything behind my back like Wiley said."

"No, I wouldn't."

He looked up. "But let's get something straight right now."

Shannon's anger began to cool. "What's that?" she asked warily.

"I'm not spending my married life beating men off of you with a stick."

"What?"

"You apply for Wiley's job and become the boss, or I might not be responsible for what happens to the next little turkey who tries to harass you."

The statement was so outrageous, she could only stare.

Getting no response, Luke shook his head in frustration and paced around the room.

She finally found her voice. "Luke, you can't be angry with me because of what Wiley said and did."

"I'm not angry," he answered furiously.

"Just crazy," she muttered.

"You make me crazy," he answered.

For some reason, that pleased her. "I do?"

"Since the day we met, you've been making me crazy." He gave her a disgruntled look. "I wanted to be a hermit. I wanted to hole up on my place with plenty of land around me and never see anybody, but you wouldn't let me. You kept showing up, cajoling, persuading, fainting at my feet."

"I didn't faint on purpose," she said vaguely, wondering where he was going with this.

"You dragged me kicking and screaming back into the human race."

The mental image of her dragging him anywhere was hilarious. "Luke, are you kidding?"

He stopped, and his hands fell to his sides. "I didn't want to fall in love with you, but I did."

Her mouth dropped open. She couldn't have been

more surprised if he'd pulled out a hammer and rapped her on the head. "You love me?"

"Yeah." He sighed like it was a grievous burden. "I've never been in love before. I guess that's why I'm so slow at it. It took me a while to figure it out. In fact, I didn't figure it out until about five minutes after you drove off this afternoon."

"Now you tell me!"

"Better late than never," he said, holding out his arms.

She ran into them, meeting his lips with hers, kissing him until they were both breathless.

"I love you, too, Luke. It seems like I have for weeks now."

"Yeah, I finally started to see that today." He picked her up and sat on the sofa with her in his lap.

She looped her arms around his neck. "What do you mean?"

"Like I said, I'm slow. I realized you love me because you're so passionate about the things you love, the land, the jungle of plants in this place, your family, your job. The way you responded to me today."

Shannon felt a blush climbing her cheeks, and he kissed her, laughing softly.

"Then, when I realized you might have become pregnant, I had some kind of flashback to what happened with Dad and Catherine, and I went even crazier."

"I noticed." Relief washed over her. She could put all this in perspective now. His high-handed proposal had been an attempt to deal with an emotion he'd never known before. Love for her. She thought she could probably forgive him for that.

"I thought you were meddling," he said. "In my face all the time about what I needed to do with the Crescent, with my family, my grudge. My life. Today I understood you've been doing that because you love me. You get involved in the things you love. I was too self-involved to see it, but you forced me back to life." He nuzzled her neck. "Thanks for rescuing me from becoming a hell of a bastard."

Her lips trembled as she kissed him. "You're welcome. It was my pleasure."

"You can rescue the Crescent now, turn it into a dude... I mean *guest* ranch, or fill the house up with babies. Whatever you want."

Shannon smiled. Someday soon, she would tell him about the strange visions she'd had in that house. She knew he would understand. She cupped his face with her hands. "I want you," she said.

Tears trembled on her lashes, and he reached up to brush them away with his callused thumb. "So, you'll marry me, then?" he asked.

"If you're sure you're ready to end your bachelor days."

His lips settled on hers. "Only for you, Shannon Kelleher. Only for you."

**brings you four very special weddings to
remember in our new series:**

True love is worth waiting for....

Look out for the following titles by some of
your favorite authors:

August 1999—SHOTGUN BRIDEGROOM #3564
Day Leclaire
Everyone is determined to protect Annie's good name and ensure
that bad boy Sam's seduction attempts don't end in the
bedroom—but begin with a wedding!

September 1999—A WEDDING WORTH WAITING FOR #3569
Jessica Steele
Karrie was smitten by boss Farne Maitland. But she was
determined to be a virgin bride. There was only one solution:
marry and quickly!

October 1999—MARRYING MR. RIGHT #3573
Carolyn Greene
Greg was wrongly arrested on his wedding night for something he
didn't do! Now he's about to reclaim his virgin bride when he dis-
covers Christina's intention to marry someone else....

November 1999—AN INNOCENT BRIDE #3577
Betty Neels
Katrina didn't know it yet but Simon Glenville, the wonderful doctor
who'd cared for her sick aunt, was in love with her. When the time
was right, he was going to propose....

Available wherever Harlequin books are sold.

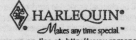

Makes any time special.™

Look us up on-line at: http://www.romance.net   HRWW

If you enjoyed what you just read,
then we've got an offer you can't resist!

Take 2 bestselling
love stories FREE!
Plus get a FREE surprise gift!

Harlequin Romance®

REBEL Brides

Two rebellious cousins—and the men who tame them!

Next month **Susan Fox** brings you a stunning sequel to **To Claim a Wife.**

Sparks fly as Maddie finally meets her match in the irresistibly gorgeous Lincoln Coryell!

Look out in July 1999 for:

TO TAME A BRIDE (#3560)

Maddie St. John is everything **Lincoln Coryell** dislikes in a woman—she's glamorous, socially privileged and devotes all her time to looking good! But when they're unexpectedly stranded alone together, Linc sees a whole new side to Maddie—and realizes he could be the man to tame her!

Available in July 1999, wherever Harlequin books are sold.

HARLEQUIN®
Makes any time special.™

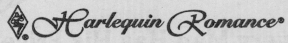

Harlequin Romance®

Coming Next Month

#3563 MAKING MR RIGHT Val Daniels
Giving Parker Chaney advice on how to become her sister's Mr Right
was hard for Cindy when she herself had been secretly in love with him
for years! But soon Parker seemed more interested in what *she* was
looking for in a husband. Could Cindy hope to be more than the sister
of the bride after all?

#3564 SHOTGUN BRIDEGROOM Day Leclaire
Seven years ago Sam was going to elope with Annie; instead he was run
out of town. Now he's back, and he wants Annie. But the whole town is
determined to protect her good name, and ensure that Sam doesn't
have his wicked way with Annie until they are married!

White Weddings: *True love is worth waiting for...*

#3565 BRIDE INCLUDED Janelle Denison
Eleven years ago Seth left Josie brokenhearted—and pregnant! Now
he's back—to claim not only Josie's family home but Josie, too! It
seems her father gambled both on a game of cards! Now Josie must
either give up her home or marry a man she told herself she no longer
cared about.

Back to the Ranch: *How the West is won...and wooed!*

#3566 THE DADDY DILEMMA Kate Denton
Attorney Mackie Smith sets out determined to win custody of
Gordon Galloway's little daughter on behalf of his ex-wife. But it is
hard keeping her mind on the job when she realizes that adorable baby
Ashley *belongs* with her even more adorable daddy—and that she's
fallen for them both!

Daddy Boom: *Who says bachelors and babies don't mix?*